BHOPAL DANCE
Jennifer Natalya Fink

a novel

Foreword by Mary Caponegro

TUSCALOOSA

FC2 is an imprint of The University of Alabama Press
Inquiries about reproducing material from this work should be addressed to
the University of Alabama Press

Book Design: Publications Unit, Department of English, Illinois State
    University; Director: Steve Halle, Production Assistant: Haley Varnes
Cover Design: Lou Robinson
Typeface: Garamond

Library of Congress Cataloging-in-Publication Data
Names: Fink, Jennifer Natalya, author. | Caponegro, Mary, 1956- writer of
    foreword.
Title: Bhopal dance : a novel / Jennifer Natalya Fink ; foreword by Mary
    Caponegro.
Description: Tuscaloosa : FC2, [2018]
Identifiers: LCCN 2017044113 (print) | LCCN 2017045260 (ebook) |
ISBN
    9781573668750 (ebook) | ISBN 9781573660648 (softcover)
Subjects: LCSH: Bhopal Union Carbide Plant Disaster, Bhopal, India,
    1984—Fiction. | India—Politics and government—20th century—Fiction. |
    Environmentalists—Fiction. | GSAFD: Historical fiction.
Classification: LCC PS3606.I54 (ebook) | LCC PS3606.I54 B48 2018
(print) |
    DDC 813/.6—dc23
LC record available at https://lccn.loc.gov/2017044113

For Nadia Sohn Fink

And for my revolutionaries past (Robert Blanchon, José Esteban Muñoz, Nancy Ring, and Lawrence Steger), present, and future

No, no, no! Come, let's away to prison.
We two alone will sing like birds in the cage.
—William Shakespeare, *King Lear*

And you may ask yourself
Well . . . how did I get here?
—Talking Heads, "Once in a Lifetime"

CONTENTS

FOREWORD

by Mary Caponegro

THERE IS SOMETHING ADDICTIVE about Jennifer Natalya Fink's novel *Bhopal Dance*. Its rhythms, its rawness, its alluring form. The gravity of its subject matter. The worst industrial disaster on record serves as a catalyst for this arresting, iconoclastic novel. Its objective is not, as several works of contemporary litera-ture have done, to focus on the victims of the disaster and its direct and devastating effects. It chooses instead to focus on a peripheral effect of this tragedy; i.e. how it galvanizes a group of posturing young people (not long ago university students), who commit themselves wholeheartedly, and whole-bodily, to dissent, assigning themselves the right to take retribution against corporate irresponsibility into their own hands, regardless of the consequences.

Through skillful manipulation of point of view, we are privy to their passions, their delusions, their self-involvement, all somehow melded in their need not quite to *save* the world, but to react to it, marking it with a bold, enduring statement. Cordelia, who is the novel's core, explains succinctly: "As inevitable as our love triangle was the need to blow something up." Thus do Ian, Caren, and Cordelia embrace indoctrination, weaponize their wills against corporate corruption, and entangle one another in a high-stakes scheme.

The narrative hovers over its protagonists with a caressive intimacy—coupled with an unsparing, incisive irony. Scratch an altruist, get a narcissist, I believe the saying goes. Analogously, scratch an ecoterrorist, get an egotist? By extrapolation, the narrative sweeps over the last half century of North America, dwelling in a cultural border-zone that presents Canada in illuminating—and entertaining—contrast to the United States; against the yet broader backdrop of the West in its ever-problematic relation to what was regularly referred to as "the third world." (Ian bristles at this nomenclature, and the reader concurs, but can simultaneously infer that all Ian's critiques are ego-saturated.) Fink immerses us in the ethos of the freewheeling '70s, still resonating with the '60s, and sneaking up on the '80s, finally zeroing in on the night of December 2, 1984, when methyl isocyanate wreaked devastation in Madhya Pradesh. In its wake, we witness the radicalization of three individuals who cathect with that event as if their destiny, and cement their identity by merging into a single organism, "a revolution of three," as they put it.

They exhibit missionary zeal, and indeed their trio consists of a minister's daughter and two doubting Jews, or if you divvy identity differently, two Canadians and one American. Political insurrection becomes their new religion, and sexual revolution, as we might expect, goes with the territory. We are reminded, with great authorial cunning, that this was a time when theorizing desire was as prevalent as desire itself, and thus ideology and sexuality go hand in hand. These characters are ambitiously, and often unctuously, steeped in ideology, and the power issues they intellectualize are conveniently not fully conscious to them in their intimate and messy interpersonal dynamics. Though no member of this trio contemplates a conventional marriage vow, "Till death do you part" is implicit in their three-way ideological commitment.

This summons to the reader images of the Symbionese Liberation Army, the Manson family, the Baader-Meinhof Group, etc., but none of these is the right paradigm for this particular ménage à trois. Fink prompts our memory to do a grand sweep over counterculture and establishment. That particular era of political and cultural ferment, starting before Tricky Dick and continuing through the Reagan years, is reconstituted before our eyes, eliciting by turns nostalgia, bemusement, and repulsion. Fink doesn't give us politics exclusively; she steeps us authoritatively in popular culture: everything from music to fashion to cuisine.

Meanwhile the prose, always arresting, succeeds in being both wild and controlled. In fact, the language that lures the reader in *Bhopal Dance* is every bit as subversive as its characters: supple, salacious, sardonic; sometimes willfully puerile and other times covertly poignant, generating a pathos that comes at the reader obliquely, and lingers, creating both sympathy and skepticism, never precluding comedy. At all times the language resists the instant gratification of conventional prettiness, opting instead for a riskier alliance with beauty, such that the reader is swept up into a field of perpetual linguistic creativity: an eros of language infused at every moment with playfulness, offering lyrical gestures where one would least expect. The author dares us to be complicit with her imagery, valorizing that which is taboo and goading us to take the bait of titillation or capitulate to squeamishness.

In short, this novel revels in blowing up propriety with the same revolutionary fervor as its protagonists might detonate a building.

And yet the very act that unites our trio of protagonists must pull them apart; thus lovers whose mission entailed a willingness to meld into one must eventually negotiate separation, which takes various forms: the walls of prison and the yet more final wall of mortality. Even uterine walls, site of primal bonding, seamless blending, cannot ultimately forestall separation. Cordelia must reckon in triplicate with separateness. But even such tragic circumstances do not preclude the comic, given Fink's inventiveness. What more persuasive way to literalize solipsism than to immure a character in prison—"with only a toilet to talk to"? What other work of fiction would dare to be so crudely creative with an interlocutor as Fink is with the donut-holed Jerome?

And as you might imagine, an interlocutor would be extremely useful, given the events that embroiled the country in the decades following the Bhopal tragedy. Fink's capacious arc gives us glimpses of the turn of the twenty-first century and beyond: 9/11 and its consequences, the wars in Afghanistan and Iraq—all of which are perceived by aging radicals whose agency, once ostensibly collective and infinite, becomes vastly differentiated and strictly confined. Readers who encounter this provocative novel amid our current political tumult will find its concerns to be quite resonant, and will be galvanized by its perceptiveness, inventiveness, and audacity.

BHOPAL DANCE

1

PETTING ZOO

I HATE ALL PETS. And even more their owners. Scooping poop, talking ootsie-wootsie, fawning and foofing over hoofs and teeth that would, will, should devour said owner the moment she dies. You pets: you're pashas, scamming evolution. Hey, look what I got: free eats, free shelter, free noncopulatary affection. Why, you'd trade it all for three hots and a cot. Not even hots: dry food, wet food, Beggin' Strips, premasticated and eons removed from blood from veins from glorious hunt. Willing woolly prisoners.

You pets are fools, but you "owners" are worse:

Hi! I'm incapable of love.

Hi! I can only respond to those who cannot speak.

Hi! I need to own—literally **own**! That's *their* word for it, not mine—

And you know how I feel about ownership, personal prepositions. Mine, yours.

So possessive, so *owny*.

All of it—the puppy-training courses more rigorous than Oxford, the fur-lined pet beds and doggy daycare, and oh yeah, feline past-life regression therapy: all a grand and tacky lie, a claim far beyond mere anthropomorphizing, beyond projection, beyond even the first-world privilege of dogs who can't breathe properly through their overbred noses eating better than three fourths of the human world, yes, even beyond some drifting humanism lapping into the lurv of them animals: the unspoken, unspeakable claim: **this is my child.**

Ian had a dog, his childhood buddy, a willing foil. Caren of course had cats, a brother-sister pair, many-toed, incestuous, named Jean-Paul and Simone. Well, you know what Adorno said about pets and fascism. "Es gibt kein richtiges Leben im falschen." Pardon my French. Yup, it's the dreaded Hitler analogy. No right life in the wrong life. Translate: no good Nazis. Now, you know you lose automatically if you invoke the big "H": Hitler. Hierarchy. Harvard. I could never figure out a way to comment (tactfully of course) on their pet love, Ian "hey budding" his bitch (named Bitch), the resistance to public goopiness masking a world of private effusions. I caught him mid-effusion once when he didn't hear me come in, hey Bitchy-witchy arwent you my tookie-wookie bitchmobile. Whereas Caren was one big furball of catlove, oh Veal, oh my dearest chop, oh Squealie Vealie, tempered with maternal reprimands: Veal Q. Chop, how dare you pee on the carpet! Mummy is MOST disappointed, all of it in a slightly East Ontario-via-North Québec clip. And I would look away, embarrassed: For her? For Veal? Bitch?

Your pet hates you, is (worse) indifferent to you, is absolutely not your flesh, your blood, your best fucking friend. You are its next meal. You are inert. You smell bad. At best you are a food delivery system, a sort of limp dildo facilitating its pleasure. Mmmrowoof. Pet away, Ian, Caren.

I want to tell you next about my favorite sweater. I loved them all: they were my children. They smelled like children. It's okay for things to take time; we'll get back to sex and pets and revolution. Eventually. But like all mothers, I harbored a favorite—turquoise, tight, thin light wool. A Protestant Jesus, who loved my particular self. Her red hair clung to it. I could hardly look. I couldn't see, I wouldn't stop. Staring.

I need help, I thought. This is . . . crazy. Sick. A, what do they call it? Fetish. I pronounced it the French Canadian way, the way Caren did. Fetîsh. And filed it among my other admissions deep in some sullen drawer.

Sullen, let's follow that word. You know definition 1:
Gloomy, bad tempered.

But this sullen was closer to definition 2:
Especially of water: slow moving, "rivers in sullen flood."

Love that tension between the manic rush of flood and the dogged bad temper of the river. Time stopped even as it is propelled. Forward?

Prey rustles, oblivious; owl freezes. Everything still and then—

and so I waited below your crate of folded sweaters. Sullen.

Caren had seven cats, one of which, she'd discovered in a past-life regression, had been a German industrialist before the First World War. We renamed him Karl (né Thumper).

Karl was a castrated tabby, but he certainly performed his ablutions with a pre-war German industrialist's passion. I had a German watch, a silver Breitling from my father's conquest. I renamed it Karl. Caren was renaming and past-life regressing everything that month: cats and people and scarves. Soon Ian followed suit. But he had bigger fish to fry than ball-less tabbies. Let's call us the Equality Avengers. No—let's call us the Purple Russians. In a past life, we were all White Russians. In a past life, I didn't love your sweaters. Not even the turquoise one.

Bhopal

How do you pronounce it? Bho-PALL? BO-Paul? Bo-Pal? As inevitable as our love triangle was our need to blow something up. Anything? Not too overly symbolic, said Ian when the Pentagon was proposed. But it's historical, Caren parried. And spiritual. (She probably had a past life regressed for it already.) Needs to be doable, I reminded them, ever the practical owl.

Ian writes a song:
Union Carbide
Don't tan my hide
You're a petrochemical menace
Far worse than Dennis

(explosion sound)

Afterward:
I felt feathers in new places.
I went to a ballet class for the first time in five years and did perfect triple pirouettes en pointe. My feet itched.

II

BHOPAL TIME

YOU WAKE WITH THE CRYING FEELING and you to try to shake it, you shake your head wet doggy-like as if that would help, as if anything would help, you woke too early, right before five, and now it's ten, and now you're too sad to speak, to eat, to do anything except—is this wallowing? You're too depressed to think. To speak, to wallow. There's no content: just the crying feeling. Swallow. Ian sees you crumpled there in your purple shirt, his shirt actually that you've colonized, and he pets your head, you make a pet sound, mew mewl, then you slide into him knowing/ hoping soon he'll be in you.

Ian said, "I'm a man out of time," and boy did he like the way that sounded. Out of time: not behind or ahead but beyond, above, torn from. A floating quality. He said it aloud, a clove cigarette newly lit doing the opposite of dangle, mouth so pink.

Yeah, a man out of time. He could picture it: everyone in time, in their apartments and houses, cleaning the yard, making breakfast, making love. Doing the dishes. Doing work. Doing The Man's bidding. And there he was, apart from the torpor, arms folded, clove cigarette poised. Apart. Still. Perfect. Well, he couldn't say that last part, but he knew it. Would this be a good topic for the next meeting? For the girls, and Sam? Hard to say. If he was a man out of time, what were they? Or should he stick with what he'd planned: the sleeping power of the poor and . . . the time of revolution! That's it: link his own out-of-timeness to the revolutionary moment, which only he could see because only he was out of time. He dragged deep on the cigarette, exhaled a pumpkin pie's worth of clove. That'll be the first line: personal, simple, true. **I'm a man out of time.**

He scratched his arm. So hairy he was beneath his waffle weaves, so beasty. A rugged man out of time.

She awakens in panic. In time. She smells herself before awake. Blood and sweat: frozen terror. Her eyes sealed shut, refusing to open. ***Cordelia, darling.***

"Wake up." He is snuggling against her, suffocating her back. His hand, his hard-on, his breath. She sputters awake, meeting the panic, pushing him off, in the bathroom barfing it all out, and yes now her eyes are fully and absolutely opened. Where is my father? Where is day?

This day breaks blue and cold and unforgiving and you and I are together in it. If I lose you, I will always be alone. She, I, thought that.

But events took precedence. That's how Ian thought of it later, afterward. You can have the most perfect talk prepared: man out of time, revolutionary moment, etc. etc. etc., everything pitch-perfect, a clean pink shirt to boot, and then whoosh, events occur to show you hey, you are in and out of time at the same time, man. Bhopal.

Disaster. A feeling more than a thing. I mean, what is a disaster? An event, a blot, an erasure. The opposite of detail. Epochal. A thing out of time.

The news came early. A disaster, chemicals, plant. December 2–3, 1984.

Q: Wait—2, or 3? How can it have two dates?

A: It began in the night, bled into the next day. A silent bleed. A new word: Bhopal. A place no one had heard of. A place that became a disaster. A blot. Dark matter. Dozens of people, hundreds of people, thousands. Maybe more. The number kept changing. Gas, explosion, almost the bomb, not the bomb, maybe worse than the bomb? A place in India, not Bombay or Calcutta or anywhere that showed up in articles about poverty or Gandhi. Bhopal: The "h" is silent.

Of course it's an American company, of course it has a squalid Midwestern name like Union Carbide. Ian unsurprises it, makes it known, common, (almost) predicted and predictable. Of course. I mean, they're headquartered in *Connecticut*.

III

[GAP OF THIRTY YEARS]

IV

CORDELIA IN PRISON

TAKE TOILETS.

You don't spend your day thinking about the loo, now do you? That's because you don't share a bedroom with your bathroom. Try spending the night the day the cold night after in an eight-by-eight with a toilet.

Mine talks, but that doesn't do anything for the smell. Jerome (that's his Christian name, for the lion-bitten saint) talks and stinks more than any appliance I've ever met. He has only two topics: heat and ass.

Heat

Because as you may know, porcelain is cold-blooded, so he is sensitive to the slightest fluctuation of temperature in our dank little cell. Our cell: I think of it as an organism. A smelly amoeba. Single-celled, inimitable. It's all the same squalor to me, freeze or fry, but Jerome loathes cold, and stops right up when it hits

45 degrees Fahrenheit or lower. Fahrenheit: we're in America, alrighty. Well, 45 isn't really cold; it's not even the freezing point. But Jerome won't budge: he needs 46+ or else no dice, no flush.

Ass

Because, well, because he's a toilet. A toilet whose seat crawls at the touch of flesh.

"Not all flesh," Jerome corrects. "Just ass flesh. I fancy elbows."

Elbows? On a toilet seat? At first I thought it odd that a toilet would dig elbows, but Jerome enlightened me:

"Actually, we all fancy elbows. People assume because we're toilets that we like ass, that ass is our nature, our destiny. Well, to hell with all you asses."

Fat ass fat ass. I'm ignoring Jerome.

Jerome, are you listening?

If you were, you might ask me how I got here.

How did I get here? Great question, Jerome. That one deserves at least two flushes. Were you to inquire further as to why I have stayed (note that formal syntax), I would bequeath you a third flush; maybe—be still, my parsimonious heart!—a fourth. Bequeath, bequest.

"Bequest": an odd word. It implies death. A vanished donor.

But it began with a bequest.

No, not request. *Be*quest.

I lied. Not about the sticking; about everything starting with the bequest. It began before that, with a decoration. Many of the 'mates choose to decorate their Jeromes, with pink lace doilies, teenage rock stars, photos of their favorite daughters. It's all down the toilet now! (It's a private joke between Jerome and me.) The real reason for the advanced interior design of the toilet is that nothing is allowed on the walls in here. Strictly forbidden. So it's our only chance for display, for those wonderful performances of identity for which the human species is so renowned.

But I prefer an empty canvas, white on white, a masterpiece of Zen minimalism. And so does Jerome.

Sometimes I wonder what Aunt Veal's Jerome would display. (Yes, we named Caren's cat for her; their fur was a similar orange.) A picture of her guru, Le Pierre, the famous shot with the cigar hanging out of his petite lips à la Groucho Marx? Or just a donut of quotes? Or most Vealish of all, nothing but a quote of her own, unattributed. What would it be?

"The imprisoned are the freest: They no longer fear the bar."

"The dead. Always the dead. And their hats and umbrellas."

Jerome enjoyed that one when I read it aloud to him; gave a little gurgle.

Or my personal favorite:

"Every representation unintentionally exceeds its intent. And every representation contains a hole, a lack, a failure: incompletion."

This is of course the problem those minimalist painters struggled with, with their brave empty white canvases that always implied a representation, were representations, and hence created an aureole of lack and excess all the more powerful for the absence of imagery. But my Jerome is a perfect representation. Devoid of excess, lacking lack. Because he fails to promise the cheap thrills of conjuring.

Prison so empty and full. Bloated with itself. Drowning in its own juices. The entrance floods you with invisible bread. Your mouth pictures a brick oven full of golden loaves, just out of sight. It's a tad too yeasty to be pleasant. Then there is the sign in the rec room, a gray affair that's a cross between an elementary school library and, well, a prison rec room.

The sign, like all the signs here, is printed in that font that screams 1950s typewriter: blocky small letters, too close together. `Haircuts are given monthly. Inmates are to sign up HERE` (why all caps?) `two weeks in advance. Haircuts must take no more than twenty min- utes. Inmates who request special attention from the hairdresser will be reprimanded and may lose haircutting privileges altogether. Hairdressers found indulging special re- quests` (I imagine the sordid possibilities: a blow job for a Jheri curl? Well, that's trading up, sister!) `will no longer be hired by Concordance Penitentiary.`

It would seem that I digress, when I was all set to tell you about this crucial bequest. Prison is a palace of digressions. Get used to it, sweetheart babydoll.

Music for Nailpainting

Caren,

I was playing The Roches and painting my nails periwinkle, such a Crayola color, and of course thinking of yours, drying aquamarine on our fire escape. Sometimes I'm there again, in our cozy commie shoebox where you decreed since property is theft, nobody was allowed their own bed. No owning. So every night we'd switch; there was only one proper bed in the window- less little room where you'd placed pictures of your parents and rigged a little fist-size TV. In the big room there was some sort of futon contraption that no one ever bothered to unfold. All our furniture was dumpster derived. So nobody owned anything.

For a provincial minister's daughter, what could be more thrilling than not owning your own bed in Toronto?

The highlight of the apartment was the fire escape, tangled in Christmas lights and King Street's streetcar sounds. Gong and horn, rumble and clank: It sounded like the streetcar was roaring out of the Christmas lights, the best possible soundtrack to fire-escaped me. I would write out there, my terrible writing for which I used an actual purple pen, as I watched you in the kitchen, you with your half-shaven head and green-blue eyes. Some cat, intent on turning us into a band of strays. For breakfast I made eggs with curry powder, which you pronounced delicious. You would only cook rice pudding, would make a new batch each day, steal a few bites, then leave the rest in an uncovered dish in the fridge. By the end of the week there'd be seven. Each Sunday we'd throw them all out. Otherwise it was macrobiotic lite: tempeh stir-fired with tamari, brown rice, which nobody really liked, steamed cabbage bought on the cheap from Chinatown with toasted sesame oil. I ate a lot of secret slices. Dollar pizza on the sly.

I was thrilled by the drugstores, so many drugstores in a single block. So much stuff crammed on each shelf! Capitalism: the freedom to choose between a dozen identical brands of toothpaste, I'd scoff when I'd successfully cajoled you for once to join me in my drugstore deliquescence, melting into all these options, aspirins tricked out with cough suppressant, decongestant, O my multiple medicant joy! And I'd read *Now*, Toronto's attempt at an alt rag, searching for that other Toronto, full of my people, my tribe, more yous. I didn't know how to be friends with anyone else. Just you.

But the communist bed situation was bumming me out. You'd insisted that you and Camus, the guy you'd picked up in your "Radical Latin American History" class at the university who was an uptown druggie who we immediately inverted to Sumac because man he spread, rashed himself all over our apartment, should get first dibs on the full-size bed. We'd had a cavalcade of lovers and hair dye passing through the hallway bathroom, but this was too much. Sumac's pants, roach clips, crumpled-up potato chip bags—he pretty much lived on chips; no attempts at brown rice and seaweed for sweet Sumac—well, they pretty much took over.

I was in a fury. Every night I'd come home, and the door to the room with the one real bed would be closed. FURY because you were colonizing the one bed, after making such a stink over how we had to share! To rotate! To disown our very sleep. So how pissed was I when you confessed that you and fucking Sumac weren't even fucking; you guys were just in there watching the fucking tiny TV? I wanted the bed wanted to fuck. God, how I wanted to fuck.

See, my days were long. I was not exactly a soap opera star; more like a soap opera clown. Like a circus clown, but stupider. I came at 5 a.m. and sat until somebody put me in hair and makeup and a script. You're the nurse, you're the hooker, you're the dead twin. Non-union, so I could only have two lines in any one scene. An American enterprise, shot on the cheap on an East York soundstage tricked out as a very clean New York. The best thing about being a soap opera clown was that my day ended by 11. But also the worst: I dreaded coming home to the sounds of Sumac and you in the bed that was supposed to be ours, to be no one's. I'd get my slice and walk cross town, uptown, downtown, sometimes to my acting class, sometimes to the museum to stare into the painted faces, sometimes straight to nowhere. I had stopped doing drugs all drugs even cigs like five minutes before I moved in with you because you were a communist and thought them bourgeois and now that I had no drugs I had to work or walk (or fuck). I wanted to fuck **you**, actually, but I couldn't quite let the left ventricle of the brain tell the right, because I wasn't gay, because I wasn't able to imagine a planet on which you would want me. So my brain was exploding. So I hated Camus. So I called you owny: the worst crime.

But then there were your sweaters . . .

Caren with her sweaters, stacks of them tucked into black milk crates stacked high. Tight bright solids. Okay so it sounds absurd, right, but I honestly wasn't aware of being attracted to her—just those sweaters. Hers. Then her in her sweaters. But still not her quite. Oh, ye holy ones, ye fuzzy ones, sleeping so bright in your milk crates. I spun their wool-cotton blends into an exalted gold, shining too bright for me to notice the sexual hue of it all. To notice her. Body and crud and all that earthbound muck of desire, flesh, corpse. This gleam. It cast its woven glow on the kingdom of her worldly goods: the bronze horse figurine from a high school summer misspent in Greece, that single silver earring with the skull, never worn, and somehow the holiest of all: the toothbrush—purple. Who the hell has a purple toothbrush?

The sweaters. I'd lie on **our** purple patchwork-quilted bed when Caren and Camus were gone, and gaze up at them and feel such profound contentment. Heaven. I would touch them when she was gone. Close my eyes, my nose, my ears, submit to the proprioceptive pleasures of cotton, silk, angora, cotton again. I didn't think in names, fabrics, categories. Only touch, joy. Though she was forever brushing them off with an annoyed merde, why did I ever get a white calico, I never noticed the cat hairs. She had grown up poor, she explained, she rationalized. That's why so. Many. Sweaters. (Her diction.) I had maybe two sweaters, stolid blue wools, and a gray sweatshirt purloined from some ex-boyfriend's dirty laundry. I never "checked in," as Ian would later call it, to see how Caren felt, because I didn't understand my sweaterlust to be precisely about Caren. Nor did I think it was precisely about the sweaters. The **sweaters**: the word even still gives me that little fabric frisson.

So was my sweaterlust reciprocal? Well, my clothes certainly inspired no such passion. There was little to be said for them, poor dears: acid-washed, mass-produced, too-tight, many-buttoned abominations. Generic, loveless creatures all. So though I never acquired much in the way of clothes capital, when the inevitable happened and my lust somehow moved from sweater to what lies beneath (more on that soon), Caren rehabbed me a bit. Black is better than navy, patent leather is tacky, don't pop your collar, wear all-cotton, don't use nicknames. Don't call them "groups"— say "bands." Her sweaters were certainly rock stars: celestial, soft, a band of sirens playing out my nights. To have Caren love me back would have been as absurd as to have her turquoise cashmere profess such a sentiment. Reciprocity? No thanks.

You know all these stories. You would tell them differently, or remember others: the blow job delivered to some soap clown in the dressing room toilet, my migraines, my night rants. Oh, we'd talk all night then, still practically college girls really, laughing at the torrential rain of letters from the blow job's recipient. And some other assorted suitors, whose names you didn't recognize. Quite the aimless slut now, aren't we? you'd smirk as you riffled through my mail. This was before e-mail: a mailbox filled daily with the detritus of my messy affairs. I didn't know how to end things. Still don't.

New paragraph! The Roches, James Taylor, Joan Armatrading. The music of our slightly elders. Not parents: big sisters, longhaired brothers, first lovers. You had punk, or at least the awful local Toronto version thereof. I hated it loudly. And you with Sumac and all that radical Latin American history. Inevitably it led to salsa. I hated it silently. You had this record that had this song that went: *Decisiones / cada día / nadie pierda nadie gana / Ave Maria!* Rubén Blades, my informants tell me. And FYI, it's alguien, someone, not nadie, nothing. Someone loses, someone gains. We would paint our nails and salsa whitely.

I played it recently: I contrabanded it into prison. And yeah, I misremembered the words, I misremember it all. But close my eyes and I'm right back there. We were in this tremendous adventure where nothing happened. Would anything ever happen? I spent so much of my youth eating greasy pizza, wondering . . .

Then they fired me at the soap, and you fired Sumac and got me the gig waiting tables with you and your sweaters at Café du Roi. So we were together even more than ever: at the commie apartment, at the café, at those endless activist meetings. It's more like inactivisim, I joked. All we ever fucking do is argue.

Enter Ian.

V

VOLKS

I'M GOING TO TELL YOU about us the way I would if I were recruiting you. "Telling folks," we called it, never using so crass a word as "recruiting." "Folks": what a cringe-worthy word. Only rich college kids say "folks."

We were such grumblers. Three years of school and what? Fucking nothing, that's fucking what, man. Fuck. We loved that word. We were dropouts or hangers-on or postgrads: same difference. Three of us in two rooms. Then three of us in one bed. Cheap wine every night, Concha y Toro or worse. Camels unfiltered, or hand-rolled if you're feeling proletarian like Steve, giant bottles of Bukoff vodka Caren christened Fuckoff, which left a toilet taste in the mouth, and we knew, oh man we knew it all. Ronnie with his finger on the red button, Maggie giving the miners the finger, Brian giving Ronnie the eye. The world gone sullen. The world ready to be exploded, only it didn't know it. It just wants its MTV, Caren bitched. But we knew; it all made a horrific backwash of sense. Pass the Fuckoff.

If I were going to recruit you, I'd take you to Caren and hand you a packet of *Sugar*. Caren had started an underground revolutionary zine, *I Heart Sugar*, printed in the off hours on her gallery's photocopier. *A Zine by Gallery Hags for Gallery Fags*. It featured her prime collection of '50s ads aimed at brainwashing women. "Sugar makes girls pretty!" You get the picture. *I Heart* featured a different body part each issue. Ear as cover girl. An arched eyebrow centerfold. And of course *I Heart*'s bestseller: a hairy lip, magnified times ten. Revolutionary tracts, of varying degrees of intelligibility, meandered at odd angles between the images. Caren was the quietest of us, but brought in the most folks. Until Ian, she and Sam were our de facto leaders, fighting endlessly over what this untidy entity of anarchists, feminists, unshavers of pits, Sandinista sympathizers, neo-lacto-ovo-vegetarians, should be called. Sam Patel had started it all at university a few years back; I can't recall what he called it, but "red" was prominently featured. Caren hated red anything, ick, like it's 1934 and we're some goddamned Leninist cell or something. How about I Love Trouble? Too silly, said Sam; too derivative of your zine, nobody dared to say. Steve suggested something sorta neutral, broad, inclusive, like the Progressive Alliance. "PA." Nah, too student uniony. Until our dyslexic messiah arrived, half our meetings in the backroom at Café du Roi were spent debating our name. Oh, for chrissakes—let's just call it the No-Name Revolution, I hissed more than once during crit-self-crit. I wasn't joking.

Crit-Self-Crit

Every meeting ended with it. Confirming that this was church.

What a commie throwback, maybe Maoist, Caren muttered, but I liked it. I liked the way "self" was the lunchmeat buried between the two thick slices of criticism. The proper place for self: public, interrogated, only notable for its flaws. Improvable.

My first stab at it proved near-fatal. I thought we got hung up on the name issue, I said carefully at the end of my first official meeting (that's the "crit" part—of the superstructure, of the group: the we of me). I guess now I'm supposed to talk about, uh, me? Caren nods. I thought I could have contributed more to the discussion of structural poverty. I took economics and can actually disprove the Laffer curve in like three seconds (that got a laugh). And I thought—

That's it, Cordelia; everyone just gets to say two things. A crit, and a self-crit. Just like the name says. No more. Caren is making the off-with-her-head gesture, smiling. Oh, I thought, I—I redden, I sit. I clear the dishes. It's only a diad: crit, then self-crit. Not crit/self/crit. No sandwich.

Caren stands, next, last: I thought we could have done a better job of including our newer members in our discourse, she smiles at me and then lands on Sam. Turns out her self-crit has a funny way of losing the "self" and turning back into pure crit: I noticed I wasn't really heard during the name discussion, I felt silenced, and I'm working on not allowing that. She looks hard at Sam, who nods therapistically. **Smile.** Her face does more than light up the room; it invites immolation. Okay, we're done. Thanks, folks. I drop a glass right in front of Caren and she doesn't help me pick it up. Just watches me bend my ass in the air, wave it hennishly as I cut my fingers, scooping up shards, bussing my failure.

I was working at the front of the café, with the gay girl waitresses, each with hair dyed a different red, clattering plates across a black-and-white-checked art deco tiled floor. When I think of us, I think of that floor. I was in love with that floor.

And with Ian. Owl father. Lover. Hockey jock. Killer. But that came later. (All over my face, and maybe yours . . .)

So. Ian came to Café du Roi one fine February dusk wearing a long underwear shirt with a waffle weave, dyed an uneven lavender. He looked gay, he looked druggy, he had that black thick hair and eyes to match, but I just noticed his shirt. See, I wasn't a hair dyer; I'd gotten the peroxide out of my system in high school. I had graduated to fabric torture. Dying, sewing, bleaching, cutting. No fabric was safe. I was tormenting my clothes any way I could, hoping the dye would seep into my skin, disfigure me. So I had a certain admiration for the thought that went into a DIY lavender waffle weave, even if the uneven execution left a bit to be desired. So his shirt seized me. My one true nun.

A pink cotton shirt, unevenly hand-dyed purple. Waffle woven, undershirt outershirted. He opened the door, I saw the place where his sleeve met skin. I will kill you, I thought loudly enough that I hoped he'd heard. I saw his sleeve and knew he would be my immolation. At last!

Nonesuch

The burning nuns. Every day that winter I woke up thinking of them. Buddhists, who burned themselves to their very deaths in front of the Pentagon. **Nun** is such a Catholic word; I wish I knew Vietnamese so I could tell you what it really means. It was all thirdhand; I was too young to remember the reportage. They were in my North American history textbook in eleventh grade, the one that stressed women's contributions to the American Experiment. There was apparently no Canadian Experiment, no Canadian dream, nor women to dream it. Just Canada. French versus/avec English. Plus hockey, maple syrup, Trudeau, John Cabot. But women's contributions were the domain of the

American Experiment. And this was quite a contribution. Could I be such a one, such a nun?

I looked out the window of Café du Roi as Ian strolled in, his unevenly lavendered waffle sleeves bunching at his skinny wrists as he opened the screen door. I ached to burn. I looked out at the miniature maples bursting green with swallowed light. They were the owner's, a hothouse novelty, posed on either side of the café's front door. It was my job to bring them in every night, to put them to bed under the basement lamps, glowing purple over our pot plants.

So I took one hand out from my sweatshirt's pocket and imagined my own skin so waffled.

Ian walked in.

These moments of intensity stretch sideways. Your father owling his way through that door. Me, burning to immolate. Do you feel it? We could use the language of film and say it's the screen stretching sideways. But it's not a screen. It's a life, mine. So what is this lateral motion? I want to put a valence on it, deem it positive or negative. But don't forget about the electron, always negative. So French. That's my fear, of course. To live the electron lifestyle. Once I start crying, the task becomes how to turn it off. The more I try to stop, the more I sob on and on. This is not unusual, I think.

Ian walked in.
"I am the light," I thought.
Hey, I said.

Of course I disliked him, immediately and forcefully. His politics were still bourgie, like I mean he believed in representative democracy, petitions, voter motor drives. Only Ian had a plan. We'd talk ourselves in circles, get lost, digress, dither into disestablishmentarianism versus ecofeminism, get drunk. Ian would stand up, part the seas. Let's do it up, he'd say, smoking clove after clove, driving his white Dodge for a Fuckoff run. Clove cigsmoke, vodka breath, wafflesweat. It was driving me wild. Like, literally: I was going feral. My hair knotting into leaf, into pellet, hurt song. And he wasn't, you know [whisper] *smart*. Actually he was a bona fide dumb jock dyslexic hockey player. Actually he was Jewish. American. It felt like incest. It felt like fuck. Even then, in the now of this scene. Let's go back there:

I saw his sleeve and knew that he would be my immolation. At last!

And so I recruited Ian.

Hey, are you interested in justice? A woman's right to choose? No nukes? Whole grains? I'm involved with this group. For folks interested in justice. Change. Waffle weaves. What's your name?

Ian, meet Caren.

Fat/Free

O daughters of Reaganomics and orthodontics. Gathered here over a linoleum table, playing canasta in the prison rec room in a winter afternoon that wants to take a nap. Curl up in its own lap. Clinical green floors, table lamps sporting Tiffanyish glasswork. A '70s vegetarian bistro left forty years to ripen. Macramé sold separately. Every time the door opens light glows into us I want you yellowly. Will you have me. Today is taken care of, my codfish. Today is this rec room, the dated light, unwise herringbone patterns made on the friendly carpet by such lamps as these. But what about tomorrow? Try yesterday. Circa 1984.

It was newly 1984 and the floor was hardwood. Waxed, but not newly. This was before organic this and chem-free that. This was after the big earthquake in Quebec City—5.2 at the epicenter. Seriously? Isn't it too cold here for quakes?—which didn't seem like it would be forgotten by the next decade. The next thing in the news was fat. Fat makes you fat! So out comes fat-free fried this, double-fudge fat-free that. I am on that fairly waxy and probably toxic floor, staring at the Goodwill green couch, noticing how much cat hair has collected on my black jeans. Yeah, fat makes you fat. No kidding, I scoff to my aunt. The phone isn't cordless; I think only rich people had those then, or maybe they hadn't been invented. Outside, cars are failing to start, someone breaks something important—maybe a tibia? One of those bones you remember—and the night bites your lungs as you amble out across Spadina Avenue to get a fat-free chocolate-cherry soda from the kitty-corner package store. You are me, more or less. There was less of me; those were the skinny years, when Caren wouldn't let me order my own entrée; she enforced the mandatory split. Cheaper, and besides, you don't want to get chubby again. Well, do you?

Fat memories stroll around like stray cats, venal, hungry on Friday at (whatever time it is—we're clock-free) in a low-cal prison cell. What is it memories do. Embed? Inhere? I can't think of the word, that smacks right perfect to describe why these stick. I pull a sheet with someone else's stains around my shoulders, pondering. Our bed had blue sheets. Don't you step on my blue suede sheets, I'd Elvis to your eye rolls. And a green comforter, heavy as a non-fat-free corpse. Your bed. With your big legs attached. I made it mine.

The prison walls disappear in the dark. The toilet stinks. I sink back twenty-odd years into your bed, your room, your legs. "Yours, mine. I hate those, what are they? Possessives? They're so *owny*," you said when I asked if I were yours. Your—? Fill in my blank. A Chicago World's Fair poster faces the bed as we sink into one another. You were always one for ephemera.

Some moments imprint, they engage, they impress. There's that cat hair, soda, phone call, synapsing away in the hard-drive whoogy-whatsit in my brain and good Christ it's thirty-odd years later and I'm masturbating aimlessly (though who's to say what constitutes purpose when it comes to such endeavors) on sallow sheets.

Jerome, are you listening?

The bequest? I just told you.
You have to listen between the lines.
Okay: You flush, and let's try again.
Maybe you'll get it in list form:

Owl Dancer

I. Nobody is keeping me from my dancer. She spreads bobs hesitates, then springs, that distinctive arch in flight wed to also arched claws. I was going to say echoing, but there's a wedding in that echo. Holy matrimony, arching dancer.

II. Aching, too. Every dancer aches. As she spits out a pellet (contents: moleskull, mouse butt, cricket crust, and Q-tip, cotton missing on one side) and calls ooo ppp aaah to her mate, she aches. If we were to locate that ache it would be in the spine, a thimble of pain radiating out into the left wing and down the right claw. The net effect: ache.

III. On the make: the dancer is one who preys. "On the make" is the wrong term for this, yet it fits: the sense of action, of creation, and of course, movement, all in process. In motion. Making, made. Mad.

IV. Princess. This particular kind of dancer is not a princess. Though she is small. Watch how petite her feet are when they curl around the prey. Her scientific name harkens back to Athena.

V. Atheist. In love with God. Gauze, gaze: all of it.

VI. I am unable to hunt this dancer down.

VII. Dancers are killers by nature. They take all manner of prey. Grasshoppers, earthworms, starfish. Medium-sized moles. By nurture they are—what? Their songs don't fill the night.

VIII. The pyramid of numbers dictates that the number of their prey must far exceed their own. Otherwise the dancer eats herself out of business.

IX. A mind in a jar. Ajar. They talked about it like it was a terrible way for a body to be: a jar, a sack, inert and sad. But how great for the mind! Mind takes over. Body shrinks. No! "Jar" is really overstating it: try sac—no "k." Transparent, ghosting toward invisibility. Only pain alerts the brain to its presence. A jar, ajar. The body rebels. The dancer pauses.

X. And Jerome flushes, as if to ask, again, how I got here.

XI. But Jerome, that was my question for you.

I lied about lying. About everything starting with the bequest. About everything.

VI

BEFORE THAT

IT BEGAN BEFORE ALL THAT, when I was squatting in a field outside North Bay Blueberries. I'd been living there since dropping out of university, wondering what the hell. Yup, I was farming blueberries in the wilds of Northern Ontario, and also strawberries and rhubarb. Small peanuts. Puny but juicy fruits. And some subpar squash.

The pumpkin plant replanted itself. I'd ripped it out, thrown it in the mulch pile, because it was covered with a mildewy sort of substance all the books said was fungal and would kill it. The babies killed me: little acornlike mini-pumpkins, still green, so podlike and unlike the orange globes they'd become. I was weeding, reading some crappy magazine I'd stolen from the dentist's office that had one of those "great events from the day you were born" charts in lieu of the usual horoscope, searching for some sort of sign, some indication of my fate.

On August 28, 1966, the Beatles gave an interview in Los Angeles and there was a proton flare causing sudden ionospheric disturbances (SID). And Shania Twain turned one (Happy Birthday, Shania!) and "TV Batman" was born. Hmm. No divine revelations here. But the whole conjuring of my birth made me starved for more of me. So I left the yard, leaving the pumpkin babies to their fate, and went to disinter mine.

I knew exactly where I was headed: the closet with the workingman's lunch pail filled with the stack of photos that I'd carted from place to rootless place. Aunt Veal had given them to me, "Your history!" she oversold them as she thrust them into my hand, her nails tearing the edges of one as she exclaimed, "Awe, look at that! You were so cute." Past tense, my cuteness.

Three houses later, I opened my closet, opened the gray workingman's lunch pail, and decided to go through all that junk I'd been carting around. It was too late in the day to harvest anything, and I didn't want to admit to myself that what I really wanted to do was waste the day looking at pictures of my vanished family, so I figured I'd take a pile of photos and sit in my favorite field and weed out the keepers from the rest. Salvation Army, here I come!

But salvation was not to be the order of the day.

Who was that man, blurred in the corner? It didn't look like the father proffered to me by my mother of the many marriages. That father: so stern and quiet, a calm edged by kindness. Was I his kind? Kinder, kindling . . . ? The picture was so blurry it could have been anyone's father.

The astute reader questions how I knew the smudgy blur of man was:

    a. my father
    b. not the kind man proffered by the many-married mother
    c. a man at all

Well. Sometimes when you blur your eyes at an object, you see its form more clearly.

Its core. Its soul, or so Aunt Veal, who got religion along with her Holt Renfrew platinum card in that third and final marriage, would say. So I saw in that blur my father: a stranger, a soul, mine.

Do you see that nose? My nose. But masculine. How so? you ask. Squarer. Less hesitant? I see it. A field and a man, the border between the two blurred.

So let's begin here, with a blur. Isn't that the reality of beginnings? Not in explanation, not in action (lights, camera . . .) but in a blur. That's why I hate movies. Too much clarity. In real life, drama starts in a blur, a sort of primordial muck of images and events, out of which a something, let's call it a conflict, emerges.

That day, I walked backward into my blueberry patch—it only seemed natural, considering the blurring of it all—and saw a harvest. Pumpkins the size of blueberries. And knew my father had bequeathed me this revolution. Now, to find it.

How?

Owl seeks nest hole. Requirements: dark, elevated, impossible for the egg stealers to reach. Dry. Preferences: already limned with feathers, crunchy carpeted, pelleted. Chest remembers egg feel, baby feel; beak recalls egg scent, baby song. Now hunger, now hunt. Over there: a prime candidate. Mole. Flies up and up, trees scattered below like a field of wildflowers. Empty sky: starless, clouded. Birdless. Swoops down for mousekill. Gobble ah delicious crunch.

Now nest. Another hole, this one empty, dark, small. She doesn't notice the edifice it's attached to. It's the hole that matters: shape size feel. Owl thinks in holes not trees. Scent not species. She enters and sniffs and digs. Someone else's pellets. Owl feels at home. She pellets bone and mouse and sky into nest. Folds herself into eggtime.

Dancer

A nest of her. She rustles, feeling her feathers. Her feathers, her tang. She shuffles them, ignoring scent of twig and hawk and steel, and plucks another to add.

The night is blue. Moon moving, ready. She blinks and hoots, sound burrowing into feathers. This, and this.

Scene: At the ballet.
Well, not quite.
Okay: At the ballet classroom.

The ballet master tells her to hold the pose: First Arabesque. The other girls are dismissed. HOLD IT! She holds it. Leg extended, arm outstretched, O. reach me. The ballet master leaves with a sneer. She can see him on the porch through the window, smoking a slow cigarette, taking his sweet time. So upright: his posture is so good. A smoke ring is blown. Her fingers go numb. She wobbles. The ballet master stamps out the cigarette, smiles at her through the window. Her right arch cramps and sadness pools in her toes. She smiles. She doesn't see it but feels it: the ballet slipper, thrown at her tit. The left one. Better, the ballet master sighs, his finger grazing but not quite touching her back. **Hold it**. Over and over she plays this back. Hold it, hold it. And thus I discovered sex.

Scentbirth

Here's a secret: I like to smell like my daughter.

I use her stuff—minty shampoo, chamomile conditioner, body lotion forged from the sweat of a trillion roses—all mixed together into a tutti-fruity baby scent. Indiscriminately mixing them, that's right. Glop them together on my hand and rub it in. I run my so-glopped hand through my hair, swish it like I'm seaweed. Like I'm her. Are you repulsed?

"It makes me feel closer to her" is the stock response supplied by the Superego Censorship Council, which I imagine lives under my left armpit, specifically formulated to answer the obvious WHY question.

They stole my daughter; her personal hygiene products are all that's left me, effuses the drama queen who lives under my right pit. I can't smell her anymore.

But the **what** is so much more interesting, isn't it?

I scan everyone's photo albums, skipping the mise-en-scène, the family drama subtext, the period costumes, for the teeth. Good or bad? Fixed? Protruding? Aging? Stained? Do I just notice teeth more now that I'm going dental? (Rhymes with "mental"—right, Jerome?) I try to look at Caren's album again, ignoring the teeth, or rather, only noticing them as much as a regular person. How much exactly does a regular person notice teeth, anyway? In person? In pictures? Kissing? Do owls have teeth? "I'd give my owltooth for her figure." That certainly should enter the lexicon, if it hasn't already. Has it? It feels like it has. It feels toothy. Toothsome.

But owls do not have teeth. It's part of what makes them so freaky. See, they can't chew their prey; they swallow the little critters whole, gulp gulp glyph, and tear into the bigger guys with their beaks. Hence the ferocious beak, hence the pellet—for bone, fur, feathers, and the like, which can't be beaked into bites.

I'd like to be eaten by an owl. Okay, I know that's melodramatic. I'm just picturing the mad order of it: first the beaking, gnashing through flesh and blood and all the other soft matter, and then the swallowing.

Swallowed

What a birdy way to go. It sounds so neat: one act, so full of song. But the pellets tell a different tale. Swallowing is a messy affair.

Yet there's a seductive sense of order to it: one pellet for my teeth, one for each bone, one for all the mysterious soft bits a human female over forty tends to accumulate. And hair. What I lack in fur and feathers, I make up for in hair.

Parcels of me. How much nicer to distribute postmortem than ashes. Everyone could get a personalized pellet: the bones to the aunts, the hair to my father, fingers and toesies to you, my darling. Perhaps we could bury those squishy bits of 40+ female unmentionables with my mother. Oh no, not a total dis-interment. In fact, I'd prefer to simply be placed on top, like the Jews place rocks and the Christians place flowers. My bequest.

If we're still on the subject of owl anatomy, which it appears (sigh) we are, let us not neglect the eyes. They are their trade-mark, aren't they? Stoic, stiff. Famously immobile. Hence the strange bobbing, turning, ginching of the neck. They can't move their eyes, so their whole body becomes ocular. A corpus of eye.

You might be surprised that I don't have much to say about this. I have little owl eye envy, you see, because I already feel like my eyes are stuck. That my figure is one large telescope, running toward and away from its desire—shall we call it prey?

Here's another little tidbit of owl trivia: they sport feathers with (wait for it) adaptive silence. Owl has adapted its feathers for silent night flight, so that it can come upon its prey sans sound. Owl arrives. Its feathery silence beaks my neck, breaks my bones, pellets my hair O joy O rapture mmm raptor.

Owls. They're a little . . . dumb, right? Trite. Overly Symbolic. Overdetermined, Le Pierre would have opined. Hence perfect for prison.

Back to fact (brought to you by Concordance Penitentiary's rec room lending library): The leading edges of their feathers have stiff fringes that reduce noise, while the trailing edges have soft fringes that reduce turbulence. And to break it down, let's beak it down further: downy feathers cover the surface of the entire wing to further reduce sound.

Okay: so last, we get to the foot. Zygodactyl! Yup, that means two toes face forward, two face back, all of course in the service of prey. Everything designed to maximize owlkill efficiency. Those zygodactyls making a pretty damn effective claw. How safe I'd feel surrounded by those four, two forward, two back, so efficiently clutching me on my way to (being) prey.

Quel prayer, owl!

And a short note about a long beak: the feathers hide it. That's why we think they're so cute. It's an instrument of destruction, really, but those flattering feathers holster it. Conceal its purpose so murderous. Fascinating, eh? Oh, I could owl on forever. Because, baby, I've got forever.

[[captive]]

I'm in here for good, for life, for this particular sickness unto death. Moi + Prison: a marriage of sorts. So I may as well digress. Create new words: owlesse. Verb: To digress about owls. To suspend time with something feathered.

Is that what we did?

Is that why I'm caught?

Prison makes you horny. Get it?

VII

SEXPARTY!

COME ALL OVER MY FACE.

I like writing that, like thinking of your brows (so scant for a male) arching in rapturous surprise. "Come all over my face": a porny corny phrase. "All over" is what clinches it. And what would that solve. How do I dig myself out of this uncome covered hole. How do I face it. A cell, a toilet. Jerome. Well. Come all over my face.

The girls always look shocked by it, like they didn't know come was coming, and/or delighted, a toothpaste smile coated in come. Or choking degraded swallowed.

(Swallowing: Now that's worth a whole other essay. Extra credit. Well, it tastes good. Caramely. A simpler pleasure than what I chose.)

I'm trying to picture what my face does when you come all over my face, but since you haven't, who's to say? I mean legion others certainly have, true, but not you.

So there's this phrase: come all over my face. A command. And then there's the porn toothpaste/choking/delight/surprise. That's all over my face, too. And then there's the grand récit, the long history of coming all over my face: the actual come on my actual face. I can't conjure what my face has done in such historical situations. Right now, I'm eating the historical idea of Thanksgiving. It's a prison replica—quite impressively authentic, I'd say—of that platter diners make: white toast, yellow gravy, box stuffing, mashed potatoes, turkey, cranberry jellowesque stuff, and sometimes pumpkin pie. No pie here. Do you know about fake American T-Day dining? Or am I initiating you into its unseasonal pleasures?

I'm trying to remember my first time. I spied it on one of those everything-fried-including-the-kitchen-sink early-'80s American -style diner menus you find in those little dives on Church and Wellesley: "Thanksgiving Platter—all seasons! With pie, add one dollar." Probably this hallowed tradition started with the leftovers, Thanksgiving's aftermaths, orgies of single male customers shuffling in to approximate Thanksgiving at their local diner, followed by a long evening of TV football and a quick jerkoff to some come-all-over-my-face-flavored porn. They come all over the pages, sheets, pants, their own hands, but there is no face. This diner's innovation is a roll, a sort of obese hoagie on which everything T-Day sits. Or slides. I loved it, ate every bit. I had no original with which to compare, to judge. Only our piddly tourtière cipaille. Not even properly French: "cipaille" is just a corruption of "sea pie." Stewed meat in a soggy piecrust: meh. Caren loved it. Insisted on the unoriginal French: L'Action de Grâce, she'd chirp, my favorite fake holiday! Such a feast she'd cook, everything from scratch, all Frenched-up and fancy. "Action of grace": a robot's brother's translation of "Thanksgiving."

Ian hated it, hated Canadian T-Day entirely. It's just a pale shadow of a shitty American fascism-fest, he groused, invented by the state in what, '56? A pasty pastry emblem of the whole neocolonial deal. An echo. A bad copy of the worst atrocity. Genocide! Colonization! Pilgrims!

He had a point. I mean growing up, we didn't even celebrate it. Just piled into Aunt Veal's silver El Dorado to do some shopping. Canadian Jews generally didn't make much of our ersatz Thanksgiving, since it crashed into the High Holy Days nine T-Days out of ten. We weren't a thankful lot. But the American T-Day meal? The guiltiest of pleasures. A love supreme. I mean, marshmallows on squash! I like to order it out of season. Spring: now. Yes, Jerome gurgles agreement. Will they ever fix his handle?

But back to our problem. Let's slide away from the incantation to the afterward: come drying (yes, all over) on my face. That I can conjure. The taste, sure, musky mucusy (so addictive), but the gluey feeling is even tastier. Is it good for my skin or bad for my skin? The experts disagree. My face, covered with drying come. I don't like the "u" version; I prefer the conflation of object and deed, noun and verb, conveyed by "come." O cover me in come. Come and make me cum-covered. Cum vs. come: the great debate. Which you choose indicates a legion of erotic preferences. Is it arrival or substance. Verb or noun. A pet command, or the beast itself. You might argue it's gender, but oh honey, have I got some buckets of cum for you! Girls know. As do the best boys. Comecum O make me.

Come all over my face. I want the pumpkin pie. Fuck the extra dollar; it's so worth it. A mile-high concoction, custardy, store-bought. So tell me, where did the vaudeville convention of throwing cream pies come from? Come all over my face. Would you arch your eyebrows as you came all over my unsurprised face? Would some buried nature heretofore undetected upon my visage appear (note my nineteenth-century syntax: think Rousseau, think Wollstonecraft)? Would we see the truth? Or just your come, drying all over my same face?

Degrading. That word. What does it mean? Disaggregate: de + grading. Everyone gets an A+. Come all over my face. "All over" implies motion. Hosing. Or a hand, smearing the aftermath. Come all over my face: yes, I've said those very words (so cheesy once your clothes are back on). "So where do we locate the pleasure?" says the Professor (for aren't all toilets professors—or is it the other way around?). In the face, in the mouth, in the repetition. In the power to demand. To comply. Now we all know (even those of us trapped in American prison rec rooms tricked out in orange and gold streamers) that the fake T-Day diner dinner is never very good. Gloppy potatoes, dry turkey, and gizzardy stuffing. Little can be expected of such a prison cell simulacrum.

So where do we locate the pleasure? says the lover. Well. In the repetition, in the gap between the words and the deed. The gravy on my face.

Can I tell you a secret? I used to say to myself that it wasn't degrading; I just liked the feeling of being overcome with come, overtaken by sex. But that's a lie. I mean, I do like that force me more more more thing, but it is the stagey, cheesy, yes porny degradation, too. It's pleasurable. It resists analysis, this pleasure. You can't have it. Give thanks.

So let's move on. After the T-Day non-diner gravy come, I killed an hour flipping through pictures of men and their dicks. Amateur porn: the samizdat of prison. You can tell a lot about a man by how he portrays his penis. There's prick-as-protagonist: erect, consuming the frame and possibly you. There's the oh-by-the-way-I-happen-to-be-majorly-hung guy: full body, face blurred, with the classic raging hard-on casually placed center stage. Then there's Mr. OhmygodImaboutto-come, red and ready.

Of course, the most interesting object in any dick pic isn't the dick. It's the clutter, the clamped-on light, the dirty laundry, and the other supporting characters. The supporting cast: always the real stars, eh?

I sighed, leafing through the smeary wank mag one more time. The killed hour was over, leaving me horny and depressed and it was time to go. Oh, Jerome. Another T-Day, spent in here. What a wanker of a life. Heat and ass and poorly portrayed penises. I may as well be a toilet. I may be a toilet.

Shreef!

Just as I was about to close the semen-smeared samizdat and call it a day, I spied a blurry figure moving across the last page. It called to me, the image, and a silent sound. Shreef! Oot oot.

An owl? It had the telltale furhorns. My father?

No. A girl in a sweater, opened to expose her tits. She's making devil horns on her head with her fingers, which are simultaneously clutching the sweater's cloth and pulling it above her head. An awkward image, hard to describe.

Caren, I am wondering how to pray. For you and to you. My eyes close and your voice comes and tells me something I can't quite hear. We are in the botanical garden way out on Lawrence Avenue, and it's cold, not winter but spring-cold, that chasm between snow and bud, and you tell me you love this season, you announce it fiercely. Where are you?

This is not a categorical question. Not where do the dead go, but where are **you**? You would not want me to be sad, but this after all was the crux of our struggle: I demanded the right to sorrow, its bones. And you in your sweaters, your cold beauty, you demanded with equal and perhaps opposite force the power of repression, willing yourself the right to happiness. But Ian is the American; you and me, we're just a coupla Canucks here. Happiness? It's just not in our constitution. We don't even *have* a constitution. You laughed, picked a snow drop prematurely flowering in the frost. Just acts of parliament, sweetheart babydoll. I thought of the pumpkin babies, reproducing with abandon in the mulch. I thought of how I became you. I didn't think we could ever unbecome.

Last and First

She can't remember much of the first time; one minute they're lying down in Caren's thick single futon, eyes closed, facing each other, let's take a nap, and the next thing their lips then breasts then more are touching. Blur of sex, quick and quiet. Afterward Caren gives her a slightly sardonic kiss and then that smile. Cordelia mostly relieved that it wasn't awkward, that she wasn't inadequate to the task at hand (is how she awkwardly words it in her head). Caren suddenly talkative, wants to be clear this is a one-time thing, which of course it isn't, that they are just friends, which they maybe still are, though not just, that this has nothing to do with Ian, which Cordelia hadn't even considered, he's another continent, right? But of course it does end up having to do mostly with Ian, the invisible point of a triangle Cordelia didn't even see forming.

Later she is furious with herself. How stupid, how naïve, did you really think you weren't a threat to Caren? That she wouldn't make sure to reel you in, to her, away from him. Or something. More of a reining than a reeling, really. Mostly she's considering the relationship between Caren's smile and her sweaters. Their mutual mystery. O beguilement. She stretches under the cotton comforter, fingers it. Purple, stained: beautiful. She is something more than a sweater. She is in Caren's bed. She is in Caren. Cordelia Caren C&C. See?

VIII

SAM BHOPAL

IT IS NOT ENOUGH to be the revolution you must be the truth
It is not enough to be the truth you must be the light
It is not—

No need to concentrate; Cordelia sees where this is heading. The homemade, vaguely Indian flat bread has a semeny aftertaste. It is not enough, it is not enough. No really, it's not; she is hungry enough to devour another piece of sperm bread, but there's no more. The one benefit to kitchen duty at Café du Roi is unlimited eats, unless you get stuck working with Helen. God, she never stops: talk talk, all that folksy hey youse guys revolutionary bullshit worker-speak. She is a haphazard cook, lazy, slow. No system. Ha! Me and my stupid systems, Cordelia maybe says aloud—she's not sure. What did Ian call her the other day? Cordelia the Methodical. For a moment there's no music, no words: the absence of song.

And then it starts again: a different tune, something stringy and plingy. Dum da da dum, dum da da dum, it is not enough to drink, you must also break bread with folks, lectures Helen, ass hoisted on the kitchen counter, struggling to cross her skinny-flabby thighs. She should know; she came up with it. "Collective meal engagement." Cordelia snorts. She wishes for a tuna sandwich. Not too mayonnaisey. With celery. Or pickles. Ian loves pickles; he'd probably like them in his tuna. He likes everything mixed together, stuffs his fries inside the hamburger bun, piles on the condiments until it's a sludgy mess. He wouldn't notice the missing mayonnaise. It is not enough to be the revolution you must be the mayonnaise. Cordelia sighs over the din.

There is a child, there is always a child. Running. Barefoot, but otherwise clothed. A girl, a sari. It's three days after the disaster, and Cordelia is trying to join her. Cordelia's blond mother wore an orange sari to her accountant uncle's wedding in the late '60s. Cordelia peed all over it, she was two, and they couldn't afford to dry-clean it. The good dishes were also orange. This girl is in black and white so we can colorize her. The orange sari runs behind her. Is it wind or gas. Invisible but for the billowing.

There's a break in the meeting. Bathroom. Cordelia, Caren, and Ian sequestered in one can. She likes to watch Ian pee. The ritual of nonchalance, a zip and a tug and wiggle, and back in it goes. Yeah, it's gross. Why don't you use toilet paper. Should I dye my hair again? Red, or black?

Either is great—better than brown.

Caren says it in what back home they'd call a mean way. She just says it: either is great—better than brown. And repeats it, while Ian does her bidding and pees into a sink. I want to watch. I'm watching. Can you stay obsessed with two people? One can have some legs on it, but two need a fur coat and a trust fund.

Cordelia sits on the toilet and looks at her hand, unraveling a titian curl down to her thigh. Better than brown. There's a cut on her thigh, from where? She keeps assembling these minor cuts: a deep knife incision on the thumb, the onion won, ha ha, a paper cut slicing itself into her wrist as she opens the notebook, and then this thing on her thigh. Let's call it a gash, though that's a bit grand. Can you even get a paper cut on your thigh? And a mysterious something on her cheek, it's been there for several days, no clue how she got it. Shaving, har har. If I bleed, will I feel it. That sari girl, running. Away and into it.

I'm fingering my mother's earrings, trying to feel her. They're clip-ons, two amethysts that don't match. One so gray, barely a hint of purple. The other a robust violet, the good daughter. Perhaps if they could pierce me, enter my flesh. Holes, O, obscene. But they screw on, insecurely clinging to each ear. Easy to sweat off. Though nothing I seem able to muster here suggests it, they are beautiful. Her ears. Dead ears. Can I lose them. Maybe just one, let it slide off my ear, into some pocket of seat flesh on the morning metro. Unclasp me.

I'm losing the scene, the sperm bread, the chanting of what is or isn't enough, the toilet voyeurs, the hair-dye dis. Watch Ian wipe. A strip of toilet paper sticks to his left ball. Not so sexy, huh? But that's what makes it so intimate. To own all of him, man in his filth, the wipe-up. Let me be your cum rag. An incantation to a personal god. Such beauty, his absorption in the act. The moment. A drop, containing all the moist wisdom of the universe. This galaxy of concentration.

Cordelia tries to join the girl, to breathe the unscented gas, to feel her skin falling off her in small sullen strips, and feels only the limits of the imagination. Of empathy. Of time of place. Out of time. In another place. O to be there. Home of the cool wall hangings and elephant-print wrap skirts. Feet I will take you be flight. And she joins. Running across Bathurst at Queens Quay. Racing into the traffic, following her. Allowing the momentum of our human blood to pull our feet across four lanes. Our lungs fill with gas and life. A need so desperate so blind. Filling the road, the planet.

Sam Patel disapproves. Somehow the meeting shifts into a fight.

No you can't fucking know. What they feel, what they felt. And what would it matter anyway? Insert stock Lenin quote about action mattering greater than intent; she's already half-asleep, tuning him out, imagining the girl's feet. What does it feel like to run when your skin is falling off? Not all at once. In sullen pieces.

Sam Patel: obviously he's Indian. You've gathered that. But to talk about it? What an embarrassment. It's hard to capture how busy we were overcompensating for our white guilt, our hopeless privilege, the static facts of self. The key was to erase difference. Subject. Story. Everyone's story could only be, well, everyone's story, individual, bourgie and banal. One no better than the next. Like multiple brands of toothpaste: false choice, false consciousness. That was our rap on the 'individual,' always in the scariest of scare quotes. But really, somehow we knew that once we started telling our tales, we'd never stop. Never surrender our wills back to this thing, this impersonal entity we were becoming. The thrill of its bigness. Its elaborate denial of the personal. Of my person. So we ate Sam's chapattis and never probed further. What it was like to be born there. To live here, with the white and weak-stomached. The unspeakably bourgie. Sounds like "boogie." A slight ring of the disco ball. I mean, no one would admit to being bourgie, or wanting to be bourgie, god forbid, zut alors, praise Mao. But. It was an insult, our favorite. No English analogue. The B-word, we monikered it.

Calling someone the B-word made you a bit B, too. Sam wasn't, and never said it, didn't have to. But it was Ian's favorite word. Except for fuck. "Bourgie": rhymes with "Jew." I mean, I was from Bathurst Street, and Ian was half-Yank and dentist-daddied. No, really. A textbook case of the bourgies. Daddy draft dodger turned oral surgeon. Turned Tory. Married his hygienist, moved to Bathurst Street proper, then at last to the glory of Forest Hill. Mother also Jewish, also pretty, a '50s housewife drinking her highballs into the '80s sunset.

I cannot show you the LARGE excitement of it all: to leave my stupid self behind, me, "the bourgeois subject"! To be larger than the extra-large Bloomingdale's Big Brown Bag that Ian found in my closet, filled with dresses, jackets, jewelry, labels left on. From your mother? No, my aunts. My mother is dead. Well, that ended the teasing. I don't want to talk about her now. Or ever. And we never did. But still: bourgie, yeah, that stuck. That was the price of my exit from said suburb. That closet.

Caren wasn't bourgie, because . . . she wasn't. Can you even imagine anyone saying it of her, much less to her? Her face alone would kill you. Medusa Gorgeous. Even with her never-ending pursuit of the perfect shoes to wear with a dress in the rain, her love of embellishment, of RIT dye and Christmas lights. Her Québécois blood made her immune. Even though the word was French, the French were somehow exempt. Especially in Canada. It meant American, of course. "The States." Not that she loved Canada. Not that Caren gave a flying fuck about the French. Language politics? Seriously? How counterrevolutionary. How Canadian. How provincial. Provincial second only to bourgie as a means of wielding scorn. So much scorn to wield. Fuck Canada, fuck language politics, fuck the Parti Québécois, fuck the fucking French. Algeria, anyone? Colonialists, fascists, frogs. Caren hated the French, the English, the Quiet Revolution, the Lesage Liberals, the whole mess of Canadian polity. Trudeau vs. Lévesque: French vs. English: America vs. Canada. She is furious, yelling over the group, shutting down even Sam Patel, hijacking the truth and the light and the endless discussion of what constitutes a revolutionary moment. Don't you see? It's all the same. Secession vs. patriation, Parti Q vs. Lib Dems vs. whatever. It's all the same shit. I mean, French *Catholicism*? Really? That's the basis of your "revolution"? Your so-called Quiet Revolution—ha! So quiet I can't fucking hear you . . .

The meeting drifts: Caren is still holding the floor, ranting against the French, the fascists, the Quiet Revolution, maybe any revolution, maybe us, the room, this floor, god the tiles need a good scrub. Cordelia and Ian let her rant; after all, they're just Anglophones, Jews, Yanks. Outliers. Who is Cordelia to question her sweater queen? A respectful distance must be kept that neither condemns nor condones Francophone radicalism. That neither condemns nor condones the rejection of Francophone radicalism. Underneath it is Caren's father, right? Something to do with being a Protestant provincial princess, preacher's pet, what with the French Catholic papa turned Anglo-Evangelical. Some unsung allegiance. They left it alone. They let her unwind it, twirl it around, let its air out. Watching Caren spin it out, Cordelia thinks of the silk parachute the gym teachers liked to use to teach the kindergartners something or other. They'd make a circle around the parachute, watch it spread like a dead moth across the floor, and on the count of four, make it rise, make it fall, make it rise, and let go, go! It would float a moment: silken, alive, and then crumple to the ground, just cloth.

Finally, Caren is crumpling. But ferocious: fuck Trudeau, baisez les français, kill the rich, blow it up, blow it all up. The more violent her words, the quieter her voice. And right when it seems it might stop of its own accord, flutter off . . .

Pseudorevolutionaries, Sam snarls under his breath.

Everything stops.

Cordelia, ever the bourgie tour guide, tries to explain, mollify, moderate. Caren's moth, Cordelia's nun. Ian's plan. For. The. REVOLUTION! Sam Patel is stone-faced.

Sam Patel, I don't know you at all. You had the side part and longish locks of a lefty professor circa '73. A checked shirt with a pen eternally bleeding the pocket. The requisite black-framed glasses. (Who knew they'd be reborn as hipster chic?) A slouch into your belly, like you knew you were defeated before you even started. The posture of a recession. I knew a girl who got you in bed, Nina Papadapasomething, a hairy Marxist with a stagflated belly of her own. She told Caren you got up in the middle of an "intimate moment" to answer a phone call from Ian, and I didn't doubt it. That's all I knew of you. Were you born here? There? You might as well have been from South Toronto as Southeast Asia for all it mattered. Sam. Né Sameer (I spied your full name on an envelope with the gas bill). Your name means nothing now except chapattis covered in lukewarm Lenin. Racism could only be discussed in absolutes; nobody's actual race could ever be acknowledged. Nor anybody's actual racism. See, nobody's story could be told, or we'd break apart like the reluctant blobs of monkey bread Aunt Veal would make, their whole purpose to be torn apart.

We clung. O to be one against One. Against the State, the Apparatus, the Supreme Law of Capital. We were an idea. A renunciation. A burning nun.

No, a monk.

What?

It was a monk. A *dude*, man. And it wasn't the Pentagon; you're confusing the burning monk with the hippies levitating that US military shit. It was in Saigon: a man. He has a name, you know. Thích Quảng Đức. Sam is shouting; she's never heard Sam shout before.

(fucking white bitch)

(Written in invisible ink as he cuts her off as Cordelia tries to explain her nun, the burning, at the end of this particularly long and Fuckoff-filled official meeting, which is now officially drifting into Marxist bull-session territory.)

Don't you know anything? History is just like your pet poodle, groomed to please you.

Ian snorts Fuckoff out his nose at that one. Cordelia would look pretty sexy with a poodle.

Fuck off. Oh wait, you're already all Fuckoffed up. Cordelia gestures Hepburnly to throw a drink in his face. Ian grabs her, kisses her deep.

Sam Patel looks down. Embarrassed, enraged, en—who knows what. Get your facts straight, Cordelia. The kiss continues. This isn't some goddamned ballet orchestrated for your pleasure.

Choreographed.

Huh?

Dance is *choreographed*, not orchestrated, she proclaims, drunk and light and fuck that nun. Caren starts it, that white guy two-step sped up and punked, head down, slightly but not completely robotic. She'd seem to be staring at her jittering feet then suddenly she'd grab you lock eyes move hands around your head as if she were going to grab it. Two-step you. What made it punk? The disconnection, the speed. Downbeat adrenaline. Ian joins in, sort of, reveling in them, doing a true white guy two-step, not attempting punk, not pretending not to be getting off on this, them.

The meeting danced. Sam left. There was no nun.

The Politics of Prancing

What do the boys dream? Joan Armatrading wonders. It's as close to folk as Cordelia'll come. My toes are ugly. My toes must die. What do the boys all dream of? Caren has cut off half her hair, haphazardly. A razor was involved. The buzzed reds stand up, flutter. Bristle bird.

A hairless lass, alas. "Pigeons in the grass . . ." Ian doesn't get the reference. That's clever. No, that's Gertrude. Gertrude Stein? Whatever. My toes are ugular. Off with their heads, this little piggy went to Bhopal, this little piggy is already in hell. And this little piggy goes wee wee wee (grabs crotch) all the way home.

They are back at the apartment on King Street; Caren is doing a family nail clipping. But Ian's head is still at the meeting. Jesus: Sam. It's like he's gone hardline RCP. Caren tries the jocular approach, oh fuck him; he's a big 'mo. Ian appalled. Jesus, Caren, where did that come from? Showing a bit of the province there, eh? They don't use the word "gay" or its more formal father, "homosexual."

Lesbian, sure, but only compounded: lesbian-feminist. Which Ian considers himself to be. Feminism a sort of furhorn false ear: showy but nonfunctional. Ornament to the revolution. The fat-free edition. "Of course feminism, women's equality," Ian intoned, nodded Sam, seconded Steve at every meeting. Of course. Everyone could agree on something so entirely unimportant.

Ian is taking a piss while Caren kneels, trimming his toenails, ass waving high. Cordelia aroused, pensive. Nunless.

What kind of a family are we. Manson? Too waspy. Waltons? Ew, whitebread-creepy. You know they were all doing John-Boy. Weather Underground? They weren't a family. They were a fucking cult. Of white assholes. The clipping hath ceased; Ian lies between them, facing Caren slightly. Cordelia doesn't mind; she's had him, and her: them. She often has a them, beginning with her parents. The original them, the them of an only child. Caren is always happy to be we, to lead from behind a mismatched gaggle. A second-to-last child, one of too many, was it six or was it seven, who remembers, good at loving lots, sets, groups. But when she really wants something her way, she'll raise the required ruckus. Example: now.

Do me, fuck me, both, you, hard. Harder. They do and she's done. Recoils into herself. Eons from Ian, the best-loved longed-for son of atheist Jews who truly believe in lox and bagels. The youngest, the only boy. The older sister more capable, less beautiful, slightly ignored, slightly resentful. Golden boy born blue, gasping for breath, underweight, dyslexic, myopic, beautiful. Overloved. Breastfed until he could ask for it by name. "Want titty!" A favorite family joke. Favorite. Always expecting to be coddled. So American.

Ian turns toward Cordelia. What a patchwork we are. She slaps his face, speak for yourself, and okay, she knows this is the way to reharden. To retake him. She is a manipulative dancer, legs necklacing him, Caren left to watch.

Aftersexgloom. There must be a word for it: something German. I'm sure it sounds better in German. We'll all be dead soon. Heirless. What a relief. Relief at its most literal: a lifting of everything. Like a giant, hearty pee. Whoosh. The world is ending. Has ended. What delight. No panic, no fear. A sea of unending finality. A family in flames. **A perfect family**.

She says it aloud, and he laughs. I mean, really?

Yes.

Caren stands, full of flight. And Cordelia, heir apparent, only child, unson: illuminated. They have inflamed her and she will nun them down.

No. That's not quite it. How they came to this. To Connecticut, three made into one burning nun, burning world flying out the window, **Union Carbide must die!**

I mean yes, that happened: toenails, meetings, massive fucking, etc., but let's look closer. Inside the pauses, the silences. The white space. For they were nothing if not white. Right, Sam?

IX

NEST OF THREE

SAM PATEL ISN'T LAUGHING. Sam doesn't laugh a lot, except when he reads long passages of his bible, Woody Allen's *Without Feathers*.

It started with Lenin. Doesn't everything. Ian snorts. See no, we're not Marxists; we're neo-Leninites.

Caren pounces: -ites not -ists, eh? Not to be confused with Mennonites, ha.

Ian reddens. Cordelia quiets. Wills herself shut. Nobody notices. She gathers stillness, stems of it, here: a bouquet. On the ceiling, watching the tops of their heads. Shiny black, Sam's slicked with oil, Ian's finer, anticipating male-pattern baldness.

And Caren's. Nest of red. Curls are the effect of, what is it? The off-kilter shape of the holes in your head. Cordelia chuckles aloud at the thought. Everyone turns. She shakes her head, nothing, don't mind me, moth flutter.

Caren is in a fury, is a fury. There were three, right? Oh c'mon. Fuck Marx, fuck Lenin, fuck Woody.

Ian a second fury maybe a third. Fuck all them failed revolutionaries. Ian affecting the American hayseed so well, thems and ain'ts and all.

So fuck Che, huh? Sam still isn't smiling.

Ian takes the bait. Che, well, our boy Che stayed with la causa, sure, and fucking *died* miserable starving *castrated* in a Bolivian shithole, okay?

Sam crouches into himself, furrowing his brows so his glasses wobble. We're not talking biography.

Oh yeah? Isn't history always biography? The man from the movement, the dancer from the dance. Ian grins.

Wow. Sam is literally backing himself into a corner, walking backward away from Ian. His hair is especially greasy, its side-parted locks abandoned to the cause. Look, we can sit here and talk Che vs. Vlad, or we can actually figure out how the hell to stop Union Carbide from gassing the whole fucking world.

Well, it's simple: blow it the fuck up. Ian's smile detonates.

A revolution is impossible without a revolutionary situation, okay, Ian?

Just 'cause good ole Karl said it doesn't make it true, Sammyboy. Ian keeps his voice low, even. Folksy.

Caren is suddenly inside this. And yelling. Jesus, Sam, who says we're not in a revolutionary situation? What the fuck does that even mean? An American imperial corporation gasses an entire city and nobody blinks, right? If that's not a revolutionary situation, what the fuck is?

You don't understand fuck-all about postcolonial India, Caren. What do you know about Bhopal? Find it on a map. Find it! There's no map, but that doesn't keep Sam from commanding, from grabbing her hand and putting her in her white girl place. She shakes it right off, growling don't you touch me, don't you fucking **touch me**, and he mutters oh yeah? well I thought everybody else had.

Everybody else is tensely quiet. Sam rubs his chest. I know, you're in a rush, Ian, you're already writing the press release. Forgive me for suggesting that we should know what the hell we're doing, and for whom, and to what end, before we blow up a fucking building. Kill actual people. Okay?

Caren tongues a molar. I see, I see. So we need to wait. For that gold-plated Lenin-sanctioned Patel-approved revolutionary moment. She takes her tank top off, stretches her arms. Pointy tits, hairy pits. Sniffs.

Sam looks away. I'm out.

Seriously?

He gazes at them, apart. You're just a bunch of bourgeois kids playing—

Fuck off, man. Cordelia takes her shirt off. And Ian's. And Caren's pants are off, she's down to an old pair of Ian's tighty whities. The orange bush burns. Sam reddens, curses in another language, and he's gone. The opposite of a slam: the door left wide open.

Cordelia is the first to laugh, we pantsed him out, man! His face when you sniffed your pits—and they are laughing and fucking and knowing this is **it**.

Asses

Everyone was pantsed. There was another meeting, sure, but Helen and four or five of the other regulars had left along with Sam Patel. Steve had missed it all, had been in Montreal, fighting the revolution with his three-chord guitar, but he crashed with them for a night. Oh, what the Fuckoff; make it two, since I'm heading out to New York next, he cuddles her head in his chest, she is purring and woofing, begging for more.

Later, when Ian and Caren were out getting some sort of supplies—explosives?—they wouldn't say, didn't trust Steve anymore, he had it out with her. They were naked, stroking each other's hair, clutched together in her twin bed, sweaty and sweet. It's too culty. The way he controls you. Controls—who, me? Caren? You think anyone controls Caren? Well, shit. Steve rolled a cigarette like a joint, sealing the ends. She shook her head, no cig no toke no, no to it all. Pot/cigarettes were bourgeois/saved for sex. Or aftersex. Preferably accompanied by Billie Holiday crooning "Don't Smoke in Bed." But she wasn't having sex with Steve, so no smokes. Because she wasn't having sex with Steve, because she never would (oh, she'd tried, in someone's parents' hot tub, both of them naked and laughing, too giggly to complete the act), he wasn't quite real. Sex the superglue, the invisible ink. Yeah, that's how it was. Kinda culty.

Listen to this. He's at Ian's fancy stereo, messing around. I've got some Yoko B-sides, rare. Yeah? Steve, nobody but you listens to this shit, this quivering shouty mess of voice. Turn it off. She holds his head: So you're going to New York and we're going . . . to hell! he finishes. Also known as Connecticut. They roll all over the bed, giggling, smoking, not fucking.

We're starting the revolution, Steve, it's happening now. A revolution of three, eh? The Bhopal Avengers. Huh. Well, there were five, two Patelites, but they dissented, they were not good comrades, they were not *on* it, man. It's better it's just us three. Safer. Oh yeah? Steve touches that place, her tailbone, and a normal person would stiffen. Instead her beast dissolves. It curls up, grows wings into flight. It liquidates body entirely, devolves into green-black goo, moth mud. Beep zoom and it's alight. A whole new animal. A revolution of sorts. Steve is unmoved. He laughs. Strums. Strokes her back. Kisses her brother-sisterly. Okay. Well.

Don't kill or be killed, right, man? You're smarter than they are. She puts her fingers on his lips, shhh, then in them, then is in tears. Aw, fuck.

Ronnie talk to Russia before it's too late, doncha blow up my world. Cordelia don't buy into that left-wing paranoia, paranoia, before it's too late, doncha go blow up blow blow up Con-necti-cut. He's singing it ballad-style, warbly, a little croony edge of Dean, of Frank, of Cordelia. With a soupçon of a Yoko scream on the last "blow up." She laughs, falls asleep, and in the morning, he's gone: just us three now.

Reroll

Let's discuss everyone's asses, shall we?

For you are nothing if not a stakeholder in such matters. Assholder.

Asslist:

- Rectangular. Flat, though firm. Rotundular, is that a word?
- Horse rumpus, neighing with muscle. Too white. Always cold, at a remove from the body, like an appendage.
- Your basic ass. Unmemorable. Serviceable. Frequently serviced.

So whose is whose? Name That Ass: Let's play. What's that, Jerome? More hints, you say? No. I've told you enough. Well, okay. What's a game without a hint, eh? A flirt. A flush. An asset:

He didn't like his slapped; she did. Vehement slapping, oh yes. Caren was interested in everyone's ass, including -holes. Not I. A languorous penetration, one finger, then another. Not quite a "fucked up the ass" vibe. Not with mine. With Ian's, well, I saw—I witnessed? Well, I sort of participated—in a rougher, fuckier thing. The mechanics are irrelevant. I'm touching my own ass right now, for your information. A most moderate creature. Smooth, and rather appealing, they tell me, though not quite a show-stopper like the tits. My tits: the end of noise and sardines and something you're not ready to hear. Erik Satie is indicating that this is the exit to some other zone. Some Sundays are like this. Oh, this is rather depressing. I'll stop. And start our story back up.

Let's join our Intrepid Three on their Big Bhopal Adventures:

After the Sam Patel fiasco they walk back home to King Street silent separate. Cordelia runs ahead, is crawling inside her mind, aching to pee. The bathroom is in the hall outside of their flat, shared by three other gloomy tenants. One is taking a piss, door ajar; he's just raced in there and pulled it out. Let's watch; the danger of being caught is half the fun. The other half is watching for that moment when he knows you're watching him touch it. Any he. There's his dick, there's his piss, oh god he's touching it, grasping tight, aim straight, flush and zip and gone. Anyway, now the bathroom is empty. She takes a piss. What next?

She is unraveling in bed. Does Ian see? Of course not. That's part of the unraveling. Naked but for underpants. And that coat, draped over her shoulders, so '80s it hurts. Maybe '83, herringbone white-gray. Leather buttons. Sliiiiightly puffy shoulders. Angled in to the knees. One imagines the original accompanying big hair and pearl studs, maybe a gray turtleneck. So slimming. But it's from the dump, as we call the pile from Goodwill that some church drops off every Tuesday at Café du Roi. She leans back, fading into her tearing eyes but then there's a shadow something a rat blacking its way across the bed. Ian's arm. A hairy rat indeed.

And now she is desperately grumpy, how dare he. Dare what? Well. Not see. Her. The girl in the orange sari. Perhaps if this coat unraveled its formerly expensive self.

Bhopal, in Madhya Pradesh. She finds it on the map, fuck Sam Patel. Where's the nearest city? Delhi, fourteen hours north. Is that the same as New Delhi? So I could drive to New York and fly to Delhi and drive to Bhopal and in like three days there I would be. To do what? Mother Teresa some random starving children. Gawk. Probably get dysentery, or is it tuberculosis? What was that story your father told, Cords? Apocryphal, no doubt: Some guy in the '60s turned on, dropped out, flew to India, hopped a train, fell asleep, and never opened his eyes again. A tsetse fly? Yeah, something along those lines. Ian is pacing, thinking. No, we don't want to be like the idiot white folks rescue squad. No Mother Teresa bullshit. He slaps Caren's ass for emphasis.

Cordelia leans into her coat, closes her eyes in solidarity. And opens them fast, just to make sure. No train, no tsetse. She stands up: time for action. Time to dig around in Ian's desk for that Ravi Shankar tape. Pop it in and hey, it's just as good as a trip to Bhopal. Perhaps she'll make some cumin-scented rice and take it all the way. Wear a sari. Lipstick a bindi on my forehead. Fuck Sam Patel. I'd never fuck Sam Patel, honey. Is this whole Bhopal thing just some kind of white folks' field trip? Caren already knows Bharatanatyam, loves to prance around practicing hand mudras. I mean jesus. Let's just get on a fucking carpet and fly all the way to Bhopal. Caren takes a giant scarf fresh from the dump, saris it across Cordelia's chest.

What did the nuns wear when they burned on the mall?

Mall: a funny word for it. You imagine an Orange Julius plopped across from the White House. Did they think about what they wore? Cordelia takes off the coat. She is drenched, shame is making her sweat, is making her wet, yeah I'm horny horny, some dumb cum song goes off in her head, then another, our love's in jeopardy, baby, oooo ooooo. She wails it to the radio in her head, dancing out of time to any music. Any India.

Were the nuns ashamed? Were they dying of shame to live while others were killed in their country's name, in their names? Their lives. Nothing to be done but to burn that awkward tsetse self in whose name the bombs burn.

Burn name. Self. **Soul**?

Send it up, burnt to bone, to smoke. To firmament.

Burn not like a Christian, so others may live. Burn because others burn.

Cordelia naked on her herringbone, rubbing all that can be rubbed, moaning theatrically, too loud. All that could be burned.

Self-immolation: the ultimate untethering from self. Sometimes you twist yourself together, you and one, you and two, a sturdy yarn, and you can't unravel. What else can you do? Be threaded to a larger entity. The revolution. But what cloth. Whose. She fingers a hole in the lapel, she comes. An endless hole.

Wherever she is, Caren makes it home. A sturdy pan, a poster of the various kinds of beans, the actual various kinds of beans in various kinds of jars, a rug from somewhere like Guatemala. Caren cooks, Caren cleans, Caren dyes curtains—curtains! Who even has curtains anymore? So the squalid squat, the no-renter, the coldest of cold-water flats blooms, a tie-dyed flower in a cold-flat desert. A boarded-up fireplace is reanimated; soon logs are thrown on the fire. Everything glows. Ian builds shelves, uneven and smelling green. Cordelia with her piles of things, books and papers and god knows what, her strewing of clothes and sheets, her inability to cook. But I have other talents, she murmurs to his cock. Cordelia unhomely, deep throating him but not letting him come.

He fucks her blind in a pile. I mean literally blind. She can't see, won't leave this blind ecstasy, this heap of dirty laundry. Caren wouldn't approve. The musty smell piled atop it like the old hats and mismatched gloves. But of course he loves it, any man would. A messy whore as well as a Madonna. Mmm, cookies! A beautiful woman cooking for him. His beautiful woman. And something ragged to fuck it up. To fuck. O my raggedy queen. O Cordelia. He is devouring her. Her mind is drifting away from the . . . what is it, not quite pain, too-direct stimulus, no that sounds too clinical, gross, and it's actually not. Stop panicking NOW, she commands herself. Stop everything. Including the stopping. Shushmouth. That's what her mother would say: hushy-shushy, Shushmouth. With a brisk kiss. This has happened before, this forcing of pleasure. She knows she will come in an unexpected burst.

And she does.

And it's still shocking.

Afterward they sit around the fire, pass the Fuckoff. Have a smoke.

Kill the space between us. Make us one, kill all self, kill your TV, kill Ed Meese. Get rid of time, math, present and past. Delay the future. Stretch it so we're waiting for me, for my demise. My prayer. My Cordelia.

We look out into the night, the stars. They've moved into place for the equinox. Is there justice out there? Maybe on that one, a cool solid star with no neighbors. The light of a lost universe, who knows what's there now? Developers. McDonalds. Nancy Reagans. Plural? You know the Nancy Reagans all have two heads on Alpha Centauri. Wait, is that Alpha Centauri? Who knows. Who cares. Caren strokes Cordelia's palm to the border of tickle. Ouch, she says though it doesn't hurt. Ouch ouch. They stroke and ouch and then.

What is certain is this night, that star. Caren pulls Cordelia's face to her, noses blurring. We are this night. And we are coming for you, Amerikkka.

Then Night

Caren and Ian entangled, asleep. Cordelia paces, frets, hovers. Awake, ajar.

Pee for me. Sleep me in my bed. Hollow my bones. Conquest my monsters, bleed my tears. Can you? Oh, this is overwrought. It's 2:14. Everyone's asleep. I'm getting undressed. My bras and I are embarrassed. My bras and I have been through a lot. Let's look in the mirror. Ugh.

What kind of sundial is she? Red granite. Etched, old. To say there were weeds growing over her face, reclaiming her, taking her back into the earth, would be to understate the case. She could be weedy. What sundial isn't. She abandons the mirror, the gaze of her. Okay, let's sleep.

Cordelia curls inside him, or as close to it as is feasible on a queen bed with three people and no one's a fetus. Ecco Ian. Smelly dyslexic. Hockey jockey, fish oiled. Black sprouts hairing bluish chin. Two-toned dick with a one-eyed dickhead running the show. Fake folksie, fraudulent American, Jewboy indulged. Clumsy hands, too large, dirt-nailed, stubbly. Actually everything stubbly. Unwashable.

Into this body she disappears. The fumblier the better. She awakens him and forces him to bang her, **bang me, *now*.** Caren rouses, is aroused. There's an elegance to fucking Caren. Why, you could call it lovemaking. Now in the case of Cordelia, there's no making of love, no care, just aggressive appetite and body and O. Multiple Os, even Ian notices, wow. You cum easy. This is made crude, made his.

Ian swallows his fish oil, good for the dyslexic brain, doesn't bother to toothpaste it away. She runs her tongue across the unbrushed glory of his mouth, and in a rush of fish she is released, flying far from this clammy life, from word, from flesh even. O savior. Even Laura Nyro doing something worse than warbling in the background, even ass tracks skiing down the sheet, even fishfarts. This stink, his neck, rhomboid ass. This is revolution.

Hockeyfish, she calls him in the morning. What? He's annoyed. She tries it en français, Hockeypoisson. Caren gets it, laughs, and hisses his fishmouth, hers.

This is love. The best pet. It's filling Cordelia with certainty, with fire.

We need to act. To—to burn.

They don't get it: Bhopal. Union Carbide. Us.

X

PORTMANTEAU

OWLISH (ADJ.): A MOTHER EXCITED. Or excised.

I am not exactly a rabbit. I dream my father is the new president, and I beside him stand, the proud and pretty daughter. I am feeling these detailed feelings of patriotism and paternal love I've never waking felt.

My dreams are so flat and obvious, nothing to interpret here, just keep hopping, while my waking life is full of portents, symbols, layers rich with meaning to sift through. Actual white rabbits appear on my actual doorstep. For example.

Light grows terribly quaking actually I am having a bad day and it's only 6:50 a.m. please help send hard cash or soft pillows I love you or I could love your turtle, stasis oasis, the '90s. I am on top of the Japanese maples they are short, too. I love you xox hearts mwah kisses oh yeah.

I enjoy shitting in the woods because it allows me to imagine I'm your dog. You walk me, you fill my water dish, you frown over the lack of selection in the wet food department at the grocery store and settle for organic dry. And here you are, bending down, baggie already wrapped around your hand, to inspect and then eradicate my doo. How else will I garner your inspection? Your gaze, your frown as you inspect, different from that furrowed brow late of the grocery store dog food aisle. Here you are divining. All cash.

Money sequestered in some blurry future. Draw its outline like a proverbial pot o' gold, the kind you might find in a '50s children's coloring book, outlined in dotted lines, black and white, awaiting color. Some future. It crouches, it hisses, it slithers to the sidelines. Buried treasure/uranium activated by the atomic force of death.

Bequest, behest.

(at your . . .)

The money replaces your flesh, is, is . . . contingent (that's the key now, isn't it)—entirely contingent on your corporeal absence. On your corpse. Flesh made cash.

Let the record show a mother.

A mother, excised. A pinkish blur in her place. A deletion. Rosy and risen. Let's perform a hair analysis. Extract the dandruff, DNA, Diaghilev. Whose is whose. Render unto render what is Cordelia's daughter's. Only death can render this rupture. Please pay cash.

I'm deliquescing: dawn in prison. It's a bitch, babe. One female dog. Horny, hangdoggy. But back to Bhopal: now for a word from our sponsor.

Gas TV

We are the world, we are the children. White guys warbling, black children looking blankly naked into someone's camera, somewhere poor, somewhere that is not North America.

Ian flips the channels around, head doing its doggy shake. US imperialism at its finest, right? Folks who buy into this shit, man. Aid as obstacle: it's like an object lesson in it. More like an abject lesson, insane. An asshole's lesson inane. Caren can always top you when it comes to lefty wordplay.

It's always the children who deserve to be saved, the little brown kids, the farther away the better, not your local fifty-something smelly homeless guy. *Let's start giving*—what, tainted milk? Nuclear waste? How about a fucking T-shirt?

Caren grabs the remote, ooh when did we get cable, fancy. Flip, flip. The images blur: game shows, music videos, newscasts. And rests on CNN. A Hitchcock blonde in a pastel sweater set shuffles papers and squints her serious look into the camera. To-night: more from Bhopal, India, where more than three hundred are confirmed dead and ten thousand injured. The blond brow furrows. But these numbers don't reflect the true scope of the tragedy. As many as one thousand people, mostly children, are feared dead from yesterday's cyanide gas leak at a US-built pesticide plant in Bhopal, doctors said today, calling the incident the worst such disaster on record. Mostly children. Caren edits: No Canadians. Deadly white cloud of Americans reported. Shut up, I want to hear this, Ian barks. Back to the blonde: Streets were littered with carcasses of water buffalo, dogs, and birds. No comment from Union Carbide CEO Warren M. Anderson of Danbury, Connecticut.

Wait, where the fuck is Danbury, Connecticut? Why would they be *there*? It's near Hartford. Insurance capital of the free world. Ian is American; he knows these things. Cordelia is suddenly paying attention. Can you get a real news station, please? A gap-toothed Québécois with a stringy gray bob grins into their kitchen. God, Canadian newscasters always look like they need a shower. CBC World News: Few words from Bhopal, India, city of nine hundred thousand. Indian death toll sixteen hundred. More than two hundred thousand, more than a million . . . who knows how many are affected. Many are thought to be children. The same CNN footage of darkskinned children rolls. They laugh, wow: The CBC is cheaping out on the cameraman! Is it even from Bhopal? Or just a reel of recycled Biafrans? No comment from Union Carbide Chairman Warren Anderson. Is he watching MTV. Did he give, give generously to USA for Africa. To Bono. To Cyndi Lauper. Did girls just wanna have fun. Did Chairman Warren lose a wink of sleep. Did Danbury burn. Will the CBC report on the black children burning in Danbury. The little brown children burning down Toronto. *We are the world, we are the children*. Video killed the comma. Forty tons of lethal gas. Try to picture it. How many hockey courts would that be, Ian. Oh, fuck you. Well, you did. Well, you should know (etc., the lazy wordplay of lovers who no longer have to win each other over).

Cordelia blurs them out, half closes her eyes, tries to picture it, wafting gaslike through their banter:

Corpses. Instantly incinerated corpses. No.

Vaporized children, disappearing in an instant, leaving behind bikes and sand pails. No.

Maggot-ridden impoverished bodies, too thin to impress their weight upon a mattress, bodies stiffening into corpses, eyes open, flies filling their eyes, tasting them like molding fruit, their filth upon that unimpressed mattress.

Closer, but no.

Bhopal was gas. Bhopal was radiant. Bhopal happened in the night. An invisible substance for an invisible hour. Bhopal: unseen, unseeable. Uncaptured by lenses. Unrecorded, unrecordable.

Closer.

Let's get the paper. Cordelia flips off the TV sans remote.

You go . . . Caren is curled on Ian's lap, giggling as his hands stroke somewhere beneath her Indian print skirt, the one with black-and-tan chains of elephants parading across it. You can see something moving under one of the trunks.

Oh. Fine. So you're gonna fuck while—

Yeah, while the l'il brown children are starving. Because if we abstain, why, manna will rain from the very heavens! Ian's hands have moved up to Caren's braless tits. Cordelia tries not to watch. Fuck you, I'm going to Tatar's to see if they have the paper, even the accursed *G* and *M*; anything is better than the fucking TV. Underneath her sweater and flesh she rustles. Which bone: not spine, not shoulder. Enjoy yourselves. They already are.

But when she comes back with the *Globe and Mail*, they're eager to read. To know. The elephant skirt is off entirely; Caren is wearing Ian's prize waffle weave, the softest citizen. Pink bleached out to peach. It barely grazes her ass. Ian topless, hairy. Spent. But the paper brings him back.

Methyl isocyanate: cyanide, basically. Breathed in, exhaled. The plant was built in 1963 to produce Sevin. Seven? No, Sevin. With an "i." I was three. Uh-huh. Ian is reading aloud, editorializing. Of course, today's disaster wasn't a surprise; the bastards knew, the bastards always know. In the '70s, not one but two trade unions complained of gas leaks, improper storage, pollution, etc. Oh, and here's the best bit: Union Carbide was warned by us! By the suits, by Union Carbide's own boys, of the danger of storing MIC, the possibility—no, scratch that, *probability*—of exactly this sort of disaster. Jesus. "An accident just waiting to happen" doesn't begin to cover it, eh?

He folds the paper in half, quarters, puts it down. Rubs his chest, worries a nipple. He's already summarized it in his head. Boiled it down. Bolded key words and terms. Sloganized. The shrunken gifts of dyslexia.

Lemme see: Caren plops herself back on his lap, reads faster, a litany of chemical leaks, liquid MIC pouring all over workers' bodies—"MIC," ha. As in Jagger. Nobody laughs. More reports of MIC leaks, dates undisclosed—

Stop. Caren pauses his hand, midpoint, on "undisclosed." I can't hear any more. She leaves his lap, starts straightening up the morning papers. Cordelia replaces her.

Yeah? Well, those kids running through the streets of Bhopal, they can't fucking *breathe* anymore. This is worse than the bomb: Nobody gets to just evaporate. "Radiate and fade away," yeah well, no such fucking luck. He is on a roll. He is never going to go to sleep tonight. She birds into his chest, nests head under wing, feigns sleep. He keeps rolling: cuts in supervisory personnel, complaints by workers, mass firings by management, a hunger strike.

Cordelia rouses, the image of the hunger striker rubbing against the running children, the burning nun. Christ. She murmurs against his chest hair, loving this bedtime story, the total horror of it, the slow roll of it off his tongue.

And tomorrow it will be forgotten, he sulks. Ian folds the newspaper his odd way, four folds, like he's making a hat of it, and pushes it aside so he can fondle Cordelia more effectively. Yesterday's news. Literally.

Caren watches them, an unreadable mouth on her face. Ian recites; Caren analyzes: "I can't get past the environmental piece.

I mean, this was pesticide residue, see? That's what they make this MIC shit from. It's worse than atomic anything. They make this toxic pesticide shit in the third world to kill us in the first."

Ian cringes; he doesn't like "third world" hierarchical language. Pats the smalls of Cordelia: back, elbow, knees. *She* gets it. She's not some big-titted provincial. He stares at Caren's tits as he strokes Cordelia's knees, combining them.

But Cordelia is still in Bhopal. She picks up Ian's paper, unhats it. Reads the caption of the photo before she sees the photos itself: "Dead water buffalo, dogs, cats, cows, and birds littered the streets." Oh god. Better call PETA. A mushroom cloud of critters.

An explosion of images borrowed from Vietnam, right? Bhopal was in the same neighborhood: starving children, check, sudden and horrific large-scale deaths, check, paradoxically simultaneously even larger quantities of slow and tortured sufferings unto same, check. The photo-op spectacle of it all: children running in the streets, children found suffocated in their own beds, children, always children. See look: They chose a girl. Surely adults, fit and trim, infirm and ugly, pregnant, fat, boring adults also suffered, choked, ran, died? Well, yes. But what sells is a running kid, half-naked. Like that kid in Vietnam, you know, the famous one. Now this girl, and a pack of half-clothed children, running behind her. Does anyone ever walk in India? Well, Gandhi.

Look closer. The girl—the head runner—is actually, well, smiling. Like she sees the camera. Knows she's about to be here, in a messy Toronto living room, the crease from all of Ian's foldings giving her a five o'clock shadow. Posing. Running out of Bhopal, into the *Globe and Mail.* Into us.

At least they caught her. You know Union Carbide would've paid a pretty penny to keep that shot from circulating. Cordelia feels a film on her palms, back, feet. Curls in closer to Ian, seeks his scent. This flesh: O contaminate me.

Merry XXXmas

Caren with that stupid Boston fern she'd decorate with necklaces. It made the cat go nuts, batting beads, bringing pine and pearl to the floor. Bad Veal! Ian fumed, sweeping up the mess. Christians, Jesus. They can't imagine we don't want their shitty holiday. It's only December 5, and here we are, knee-deep in it. Ian hated it. Merry Capitalism, or is that Crapitalism? Well, there's endless crap involved, that's for sure. But he indulged Caren, let her get him a present, even got her a silver necklace-cum-earring to add to her collection strung through her many holes. O her many holes. Of course he couldn't not think of filling them.

Cordelia just went to the winter place, under the frozen pond, the sound of snow snowing. What the birds do: a glacial huddle. Flutterless.

Her hair so brassy, the orange of a chemical leak. Of a Pre-Raphaelite painting. Pre-chemical, Caren corrected. It was real, her orange. The burning bush, Ian pronounced the first time he witnessed the glorious copper fuzz of it. Cordelia saw nothing the first time, eyes tightly closed, witness to no body. In her own carnival of sensation. No room for sight. Even when her face was in it, her tongue, responsive and giving, a moaning orgy of orange. Still just herself.

You are the most giving and withholding of lovers. Even as you give you take; you withhold. He was merciless.

What? What do I withhold?

Why, yourself.

Actually that was the closest they got to talking about sex. (Caren had no comment.)

Except that night. Post-Bhopal. December 5. The papers date it.

I want you to stop trying.

Trying what?

To please me.

Oh.

An odd thing for a man to say when he's got his dick down your throat. He unkneels her, rolls her on her back. Lions parade across the sheets. His mother's Chanukah gift. Tan and blue lions. Fancy. Cordelia closes her eyes; she doesn't want to share her pleasure. He's inside her now and something else is happening. All hers, her.

Afterward he wants to talk. She won't. I'm seriously tired.

Are you okay? A little boy peering up at his mother. He is trying to stroke her back, feather her.

Fine. She rolls away.

He's left to contemplate the lions lolling across the sheets, the question of her pleasure.

XI

KILL CUTE

SAVE THE CUTE, kill the brute. You shall live, O fluffy, you shall die, O scaly, O smelly. The least beastly shall inherit this earth. Those resembling the human baby—hello seal, hi ho puppy—are granted immunity from farm, from table and knife, and invited to overpopulate. Should we mention that the worst offenders are those who neglect—or neglect to even have—their own babies? Shall we discuss the anthropomorphizing, the naming, the misrecognition of brute as babe?

Owls, we are a special case. Blame Athena. Imbued with mystery, wisdom, a regal et cetera. Our viciousness ignored, our babies fetishized on posters, paperweights. We are not your figurines. We are fierce, we kill, we'd pellet your babies in a minute if we could. We could.

You think this is funny. A hoot. But your planet is dying, sweetheart, babydoll, because your only plan for conservation is Save the Cute, Kill the Brute. But we are all brutes, angling for survival. We are not your never-had children, your babes turned pimply teens, your lambkins, your bediápered bunnies. Do you understand? Your addiction to cuteness, to the speechless youth of other species, is killing this planet. Ours.

Far worse than the charnel house: murder by adoration. To kill for food is noble, the natural order, our hawkborn truth. But you are sick with cute. You sterilize, condomize, abandon. You hate your own. You worship at the shrine of the diminutive, diminishing the planet, overpopulating, starving, straining, overbreeding. You are adoring us to death.

You think this is a joke. A gas. But it's why you have him. Why you made him your idiot king.

He's always there. In your living room. At school. On every screen. The ultimate pet. Inverted, wrinkled. A wizened puppy. Red cheeks, pasty face, brilliantined hair swallowing the whole screen, the whole world. There you go again. Ugh that voice, that grandpa condescension. Mr. Gorbachev, tear this wall down. Welfare queens living off the state. Why, I heard about a strapping young [black] buck using food stamps to buy a great big steak! Yes, he's stupid, racist, cruel, his words coarse. But it's that face, that pallor, so old, old, OLD, this horror from another era, he's actually older than all her grandparents, than anyone she's ever known. Pedophile grandpapa, she thinks every time. His features wrinkle into the center of his face, as if he's a couch that's been sat on, as if he's an asshole swallowing his features, swallowing the world. Finger on the red button, ready, so ready, to finger the world into oblivion. This stupid old asshole runs the world.

She gets rid of Ian's TV; you can go to the bar to watch hockey or whatever. But I cannot listen to that man. That man: she won't call him by name. Her spine shrinks every time, every single and singular time she must hear him, see him. With disgust, yes, but also fury, whenever his funereal mien is plastered over with "great communicator" this or "ending the cold war" that. This doddering monster, absolute evil in a bag of wrinkles. The negative image of the baby seal. Its ego-ideal. Its nemesis. Not a person at all: more unreal than Hitler. A signifier. A monster. Molester, she's sure of it, ew.

Not that they'd loved Jimmy Carter. I mean, who loved Jimmy Carter? Not that they loved any American. Colonialism, etc. Trudeau was a sellout. I mean, electoral politics, politicians. Of course they're nothing but capitalist tools. But this monsterman, this old-world Hollywood Loch Ness monster. They elect him and elect him again. There's talk of a third term, how he hates that darn twenty-second amendment. The world will end. The world has ended. This man has his hand on the red button. This man can—will—start World War III. This man believes in survivable nuclear wars. This senile old puppy. This man.

You know when you just want out. Of this body, O sunken ship. Sail it. Crash it into any available reef. One if by fire, two if by . . . oh god I'm fucking tired. I'm the dirtiest possible girl. A lesbian sweater fetishist with an occasional cock in her mouth. O that occasional mouth. Pink bud, like a very clean asshole. Newly scrubbed. Ready.

All this as she readies herself for revolution.

Fashion Fascism Flashback

Caren is making everything Japanese, adding stickers that say "tea kettle" or "butter" in Japanese characters, singing *I think I'm turning Japanese I really think so*. Ian's annoyed—muttering cultural colonialism, swatting her non-Japanese ass. Cordelia is glad Caren is done with the Russian tchotchke phase: revolutionary figurines doing a jig, holding actual hammers and sickles, red flags of same sewed into a shower curtain, T-shirt in red, black, and white featuring commie slogans untranslated. It's kitsch, yeah, Caren knows, but kitsch with a purpose. But Cordelia is unconvinced. So she's glad we're turning Japanese. At least it's, well, cool. Hip. Though we would never use that word.

Though once, drunk on Fuckoff, Ian defended '60s nostalgia. The media has made it seem the opposite of what it is, what it was: made Alex fucking Keaton some pseudo-stockbroker kid seem cool, made the hippies parental. Throwbacks. Messy. I mean, was Jerry Rubin *messy*?

"Lonely Woman" is playing loud, too loud, *don't believe no more*, Laura Nyro, you are too damn loud. And he's right. The suits are the cool cats now: Alex P. Keaton—played by a Canadian, no less—lecturing his Deadhead dad in horn rims and suspenders. Word on the street is even James Earl Jones voted for Reagan. Even Neil Young. Not Laura Nyro. Cordelia doubts Laura Nyro managed to vote at all. She'd ask Ian whatever happened to good ole Laura N., except she knows he'd be offended by the syntax of the question, the has-beenery of it all.

Listen: I'm no hippie. This isn't some stupid '60s shit. The '60s sucked. The '60s were mostly a bunch of white male supremacists jerking off to Malcolm. ("Mostly" is the important word here.) Those guys weren't rooted in any sort of . . . Ian looks past her, searching for the word, though she knows exactly what it's going to be . . . community. (That word: what does it even mean? She doesn't ask.) See, like we are Democratic Socialists—the democratic part comes first—for Citizen Revolution. Citizen implies community, don't you think? Steve wanted it to be Citizen Community, but that's too vague, too dippy. Smacks of community theater. She laughs; she knows he wants her to laugh. This is both smaller and bigger than anything Jerry Rubin ever imagined. Because all that epic Maoist shit, now where does that get you? I mean Jerry's a fucking stockbroker now. I mean do you want to start a revolution, or do you just want to get high and make a lot of dough? He stubs out her joint with his clog. Knocks back another shot of Fuckoff.

In truth, they were all Deadheads, '60s backwash, fresh-faced old hippies in tie-dye and Ecuadorian scarves, dropping acid, stealing this book, worshipping Dylan, the Saint Joans (Baez, Mitchell, Armatrading for the lesbos) then getting into the more esoteric strata of hippery: Carlos Castaneda, Mimi Baez, Richard Fariña. Laura Nyro. Ian's favorite. Little lovelorn Laura. He kind of looked like her: thick black hair, thicker black eyebrows, an unearned soulful cast to the whole visage—something in the beaky nose combined with the high cheekbones. He named his cat Eli, for "Eli and the Thirteenth Confession." But they were all guilty. Exhibit A: they traded Phil Ochs lines (Sam: *Don't talk to me about revolution*, Ian. *Well, that's going a little too far.* Ian: Ha! *Love me, love me, love me, I'm a liberal.*) at meetings. Even were known to sing along with that wretched Tom Lehrer. And yes the Dead, yup they'd been to the shows, dropped the bad acid.

Cordelia hated it all. All that faux folksy wailing. All that shiny shit.

What hovers beyond language, beneath the easy anthem.

What is black sound, hope rearranged, discordant. A love supreme.

Coltrane, Mingus, Lady Day. Cordelia the recalcitrant white jazzhead. But she never said anything, even grew to prefer one Joan (Baez) to another (Mitchell). Pure treason to prefer anyone to Joni Mitchell, I mean, my god, she's Canadian! As is Neil. Young, Ian explains, as if the girls don't know. Somehow they are the girls in these conversations, waiting to be schooled in some soft '60s spot in Ian's hash-hazed heart. Ian with the Canadian folkies, sounding for all the fallen world like my grandmother with the Jews. Did you know Elizabeth Taylor was Jewish? Well, didja? Leonard Cohen hit both marks: Canadian *and* Jewish. Yes, they knew.

Caren had nothing but eye rolls for the whole lot of it. Even Dylan. Even the Beatles. Fuck that old US imperialistic hippie shit. Jerry Rubin is a stockbroker. Dylan hearts Jesus. Caren hearted punk and whatever it was morphing into. That was how she got into politics anyways. Dead Kennedys, Sex Pistols, and the Clash, most of all the Clash, oh yeah. She implied she'd slept with Strummer. Twice. And now old Patti Smith, new Richard Hell, bootlegged Lydia Lunch samizdated by Steve.

Steve had no time for Ian and his Laura. Young Marble Giants: maybe. Laura Nyro: no fucking way. Steve bleached the front poof of his hair, the gay version of punk. There was no gay in hippie. Well, maybe a little, in an orgy, maybe if you're really high. Maybe if you're a girl. Patti Smith looking like a boy, skinny and mean. But she's too shouty for Cordelia. The only punkish, punkesque music Cordelia likes is Talking Heads. Sardonic, ironic. A kind of Canadian distance from the action. And let's not forget Elvis Costello, the original man out of time, but don't tell Ian. Of course, punk has its prelapsarian bullshit, too: it was all better in the late '70s, in England, now it's just Americanized pap, apolitical posturing. The worst possible condemnation: you're just a New Wave poseur. Or just *poseur*, half-muttered. Why, it's even French.

Cordelia assumed they said it of her, as she donned first a man's leather bomber jacket, then a tight black leather cap, then the incredibly uncomfortable but unimpeachably cool combat boots, just like Johnny Rotten's—Cordelia was maybe the first person, definitely the first girl (how she hates that word), in all of Toronto in actual combat boots, not some fashiony femmified knockoff. No. Steel toes, no arches, argh. As I live, hers were as worn and heavy as Mister Johnny Rotten's himself. As we lived.

Even after it became impossible to publically proclaim one's love of the '60s, even after everyone had thoroughly embraced Caren's punk aesthetic in music, in clothes, in attitude, Ian still clung to his hippie ways in secret. In bed. He'd put on his old Laura Nyro LPs after they made love, warble along with Laura. Yeah, Ian traded the Ecuadorian graphic prints for the pink and purple cotton waffle shirts, added some silver bracelets, first Caren's, then some he must have bought himself, but he was still a closet hippy. He cut his hair, but kept it past his ears, longish if not long. No dye. No boots. Man clogs, which nobody was wearing. Ian the Woodstockian, Cordelia thought as she closed her eyes and kissed his vodkamouth. She and Caren called him that, secretly, somehow sexily though it sure doesn't sound it. He shunned pot, made vodka their beverage of choice, though Caren always somehow had a joint on hand. Yeah, he Fuckoffed away from all that '60s mellowness shit. But underneath it all he was still Ian the Woodstockian. Listen: you can hear it, a grace note. Of hippy shit. His. Him.

Oh, Ian went along with the Ramones, the Clash, Bowie—whatever Caren was into, really. He adopted the phrase "stupid hippie shit" as if he meant it, but his heart remained a tie-dyed affair. He pretended to like Caren's leather getups, her androgyny, the startling boy of her, braless in his white wife beater, no pants, hunched over her unlaced boots, Nazisexually singing off-key. "God Save the Queen," "Holiday in Cambodia." Caren loved the bald irony, the Briticisms, never mind the bollocks, the lack of Canadian politesse and measure.

Every woman loves a fascist, eh? Even if it's a girl. Caren tried to harden Cordelia up, roughen her with a leather this, a squared-and-zippered that. Purpled her lips and cheeks, giving her that much-coveted bruised fruit look to match the combat boots. But somehow Cordelia knew Ian liked his women soft. Long hair, no makeup. Droopy peasant dresses, and yes, dear fucking Christ: Birkenstocks. Which were far more comfortable than said boots, truth be told.

Of course, Ian never said as much, knew it would be sexist to say as much, to say much of anything about how they looked. Of course, Caren was the exception to every man's rules, as beauty always is. Cordelia was just glad for her thick long hair, her curves, her Indian-print wrap skirts worn with a low-cut black leotard and Chinese slippers. A hint of blush, a touch of gloss to help perfect that natural look. She knew what he liked.

Pup Slut

This is a street fair entirely devoted to pets. Pet spas, firemen's dogs, cat chasers. "Strut Your Pup," it seems to be called, if the banners with paw prints are to be believed. It's something to do with the fire department. Firemen, firedogs, Dalmatians and almost-Dalmatians, splotched instead of spotted. It's hot, so the pets all want water. It smells a little worse even than street fairs generally smell. Caren loves it, wants all the dogs. "Aw, look at his nose!" Ian feigns indifference, indulgence. Oh, Caren. Cordelia is tromping along in Caren's combat boots. She is sweating; she buys a cheap lace scarf to pull back her frizzing hair. Gorgeous, Ian whispers. So delicate. He strokes where the lace touches her neck. Pulls off her leather jacket with its hand-painted anarchy symbol. That's better. Touches her nipple as if they're alone. Come on, you guys. I'm done pup slutting, okay?

Say it again, he leers.

"PUP," and Caren hands him the prize: a cross with a paw print on it, a cheap silver thing. "For you." Her eyes are too blue, she's blindingly goyish: he's all hers.

Cordelia barks, another stinking animal.

Administrations

Oh yes, Caren was a minister's daughter. It made for a good lede later: TERROR STRIKES DANBURY! *Three Caught in Connecticut Plot: Mastermind Is Minister's Daughter.* Sibilance, sex, and religion; all it needed was a cat to make it a sure hit.

We didn't do the usual lovers' thing of sharing stories, telling tales of our horrible parents, our supremely unfair childhoods, our first-grade friendships. Story was suspect. Trivial. (**Female**.)

No, our pillow talk tilted toward revolution or music. Or RIT dye. But Caren's tale was just too delectable; we torture-fucked it out of her the night before the night we blew up Bhopal.

The night before we hit the road to blow up Bhopal (well, Union Carbide; well, just the office building; well, we didn't blow it up; well, well, well it's all the same, isn't it, symbolic violence a form of nonviolence after all), Caren's mother is terrified, hysterical, calling in the middle of the night to make sure Caren has thrown out every last plastic tamper-proof bottle. Somebody's gotten at the Tylenol, did you hear on the news, eh? Caren rolls her eyes. Oui, Mom, Tylenol terrorism.

Poor Mère Mirielle can't even trust her Tylenol anymore, Ian teases. Cordelia numb with envy, so you met her, huh? Caren's mother? Yeah. And? Nothing you wouldn't expect of a provincial nurse.

"Dad is preaching in Bécancour tomorrow? Really? Comme c'est genial!"

Did she say—Ian and I exchanged The Look. PREACHING? Preacher's daughter?!? Kiiiiiiiiinky!!!

As soon as she was off the phone, we started in.

So "Dad" is a minister? Of what?

She refuses to tell which church, what flavor. Do you, like, speak in tongues? Lay hands on snakes? Marry cousins? Caren's not saying, just rolls her eyes and smiles her rosebud smile, her mystery mouth. Cordelia loves this state of affairs. How can she and Ian, lapsed Jews, not feel secretly superior. Such idiocy, such ecstasy, can you imagine?

Ah, the sordid sorties of a fundamentalist girlhood, Ian teases. C'mon, we want to hear about the surreptitious hand jobs at vacation Bible camp, the smutty story of a Sunday singalong. Did you tease the boys by showing a bit of leg underneath your *Little House on the Prairie* skirt? C'mon, show us your praire, oh, just a little bit. Cordelia giggles, egging him on; he gets dirtier: a pink-cheeked pubescent Caren, the prim little minister's daughter with some pimply parishioner's cock in her mouth. Oh, you're so gross, Ian, Caren blushes. But she loves the attention, doesn't she. The fundy kids are always the kinkiest, Cordelia thinks as she bites that prayerful lip.

The thing was, we already knew. Not the minister-daddy bit, but the gist of Caren's fundamentalist follies. It was during the sweater phase, when I nosed around her top sweater drawer and found Caren's pink jewelry case with the broken ballerina inside, armless, still spinning. I mined: gold.

"What's this?" I cried, seizing a yellow band so slender it could have been the ballerina's.

"Oh . . . it's from my dad."

"It looks like an anorexic's wedding band." I put it on my pinky: too tight.

"Well, in a way it is."

"You were *married?*" I twist it off, pull off her top, and try to make a nipple ring of it. No go.

Caren grabs it, twisting both my nips for good measure. "Hell no! It's from . . . " She stops to think how to say it, without saying it, but no, there's no other way: "A purity ball."

"Oh. My. God." Of course I had to impurify her that very minute, and tell Ian that very night, privately, in his car after car sex, all the details. Though Caren wouldn't tell me many. But you might say I have a rich imagination, hmm? And a stolen purity ring. "Purity ball": Ian and I loved to say it at random moments, the delicious sour ball of those three syllables rolling around. Let's ball some purity, we'd cackle. Of course, we'd never heard of such a thing; I mean later the Americans took it up, commodified it, Walgreened it up but good. But back then it was purement rural Canadian. Caren's.

Though in the wash, this revelation only heightened Caren's mystery, Ian's fascination with her swelling, his cock reaching deep inside to find the minister. He lusted for her shame, for its precise contours. Tell me. The furtive masturbation, the crimson-cheeked embarrassment to follow. O how she blushed.

I had no shame to speak of. To offer him. My childhood was feral and free, everything explorable. No sin: bodies just bodies. This is your vagina, my mother introduced at four. Take good care of it; it's yours. No lush layers of repression to plumb. But my father. My father gave me this, this—is royalty the opposite of shame? Not pride, but close. A detachment from the law. Something purple and prickly. A cactus thing.

Lierstein Coat of Arms

Surely there was an "L." Heavy creme paper, like you'd see on a diploma. And gold, lots of gold, curlicued around the letters. I imagine a griffin, a sort of feminine iteration of a dragon. I assumed it was old. Foreign. Latin, maybe. The language of diplomas. I sat up a bit straighter, "squared off" like my father always barked when I sat beneath it on the chintz love seat. It was in the den—I was distracted by its luminous presence. What is that? I asked my mother. The Lierstein Coat of Arms. When my uncle died, he flew to Israel. His final voyage, first class. Did you know there's a special Jewish burial tunic, white? You leave more or less the way you came. But more modest. So he flew. I had thought a lot about the prospect of my parents' deaths, but not my uncles' deaths, my aunts'. My mother is an oldest child: sanctimonious, obedient. Fish eater, fat fearer. My father's tribe were an unrulier lot. I don't remember any actual arms. Letters, gold, scaly critters, and that heavy brass frame so beloved by the '50s den, but beneath the swirls there must have been a crossed sword or two.

Everything could be bought. Your skin may be black but your money is green, went my father's favorite motto. We rolled our eyes at him, hissed "racist," but we knew. My father was a shtarker, a tough Jewish guy, back when we needed such a word for such men. When we needed such men. He operated entirely on the all-things-can-be-bought principle. Love seats, lovers, coats of arms. Principles weren't his strong suit. He was a doctor, yes, but more of an arranger, a finder of things: Abortions for girls in trouble. Jobs for the newly unincarcerated. Mistresses for himself. Whores for my thirteen-year-old cousin, happy bar mitzvah! Abortions for his mistresses.

Surprise Creampie

A whole porn subgenre unto itself. His come in her, it's dripping out. The camera fastens tight on the donuty glaze. Her cunt the presumable pie. Yeah, okay, it's just another money shot. But what fascinates? Her unknowing. Did you come, she wonders, did you come in me? The camera knows, watches.

Could anything be more banal?

Life itself could be created in this whipped cream moment, unknown to her, to us.

Could anything be more profound?

I look at thirty, forty of these, just the cream shot and its aftermath, and they really do start resembling pies. Shot after shot. In science class, wasn't it exciting to watch the sperm cells swimming on their mission? My father dies twice. First, when he is sixty-eight, the *Globe and Mail* published a fake obit. They didn't say it, but we all got the feeling my parents knew who did it. Then he dies in earnest, two years after the fake obit, in uncharacteristic peace, in his sleep, shrouded in white.

The Lierstein Coat of Arms ended up in the dustbin of history, aka Goodwill. But it did make him royal, us royalty. Inseminated with gold well purchased. To be royal is to be apart. A person and a title. A person as a thing. A king.

Hmm. It seems like we endlessly digress but we don't. Digression is our only progress. Digression the best cactus—oh, shuddup, Jerome: no silly rhymes, no puns, not now. We, you, I. Who exactly are you talking to? I ask myself. Well, you. Any you. Jerome. Caren? And who's this I? **I did, I** was . . . Why not say **she** for that girl, that Cordelia, young and free. Past tense, passed. She is me about as much as you are. Don't worry; this isn't going to turn into some icky treatise that makes you remember that bad asymmetrical haircut you rocked as you misquoted Foucault in sophomore lit crit.

Okay, but what of our story? Where'd the plot go? Bhopal? Nuns? Union Carbide, anybody? Jerome flushes, adamant.

Oh please. You'd rather hear the debauched details of the minister's daughter's defilement than listen to my patter on pronouns. Well, tough titties. This I won't resurrect. Instead, let's skip to after:

After the minister's daughter is thoroughly defiled, Caren sits up in bed. "Administer the Tylenol, please!" And we laugh, until we are all covered in shame, pink-cheeked, whisperless. Borrowed shame: the best.

We are all minister's daughters now, Ian proclaims with the solemnity the occasion demands.

XII

BEWILDERMENT

IF WE MAKE IT to 11 a.m., we'll make it through the day. It's 4:07 a.m., and I'm feeling like a million bucks. Like anything could happen. Something good could happen to you, today, promised the prominent wife of a televangelist on my childhood black-and-white TV. To you, today, she'd repeat. I stare at my dark cell, waiting. This strange human capacity for optimism. What's its purpose? The height of unreason, the height of the morning, hi hi high . . . I'm giggling, and listening to my giggles, audience and performer one. Am I the ultimate nun, Jerome? Certainly chaste, surely self-sacrificed.

"We don't have nuns in Jewish," Aunt Veal opined. She was the only girl in the family to be bat mitzvahed and considered herself the authority on such matters. Judaism = Jewish, and vice versa for Veal. And for the longest time, we all concurred, demurred, mrrrrr. But all we have are nuns. Fields of them, daisy-headed Jewesses in, what's that word? Wimples. A goy word if

I ever heard one. Oh god, how I want a wimple. And a shaven head beneath.

It's been many years, over a decade, over two, or is it three now, so you must have cut your hair. Cut it dozens, probably hundreds of times. Countless hands running through your hair. Black locks of it curled on someone else's floor. Many floors, the floors of strangers. And your own floor, maybe hers, another's, not a stranger at all. I'm trying to decide which is more disturbing: your hair on many floors, people you're paying, hi I'm Jim, I'm Sally, I'm Anne-Marie, I'll be your hairdresser, I'll touch your hair, I'll smell your scalp, or the floor you share with her, some her, somewhere. Not here. No contest: duh, it's the latter. Little hairs stuck between the floorboards. She finds some on the bed. Your bed. "Ours," she thinks.

This is so obvious. More obscure: the feel of your hair, so thick the scissors protest. So black. That you escaped when Caren died, that you were set free when I was imprisoned, that you bourgied right into a comfy condo right off the Beltway, that you cook up pancakes and public policy instead of revolution and . . . revolution, that you forgot me, left me, a patch of nothing, your waffle-woven past: all that I forgive.

But the hair, Delilahed away. I saw you on the news here once, something about health care, yes, the importation of the Canadian model to the States, and there you were. It flashed so quickly in the rec room, before the other inmates clicked and turned you to stone, to a game show host, to a new washing machine. But I saw it. Your eyes. Your certainty. Your hair. Gray.

Bequested

The pink room. In a pinkish brownstone, the only nonrefurbished entity on King Street. Pink shiny bedspread, babydoll pink matching curtains lined with cheap white lace. And yes, pink shag carpeting. All manner of girly doohickey scattered across the room. Every surface crawling with it. Can we talk about the bed again? Pink satin twin, with a family of pink pillows (embroidered with mauve truisms, home is where the heart is). Who chose this shit? This is the bed no man could ever enter. This is the bed of a woman who never left seventh grade. This was my bed, for the two months After. Purgatory. Awaiting trial—flight risk. Flap flap.

I'm feeling sorry for the birds again. Now that's a lousy way to spend an afternoon. Think about it: I get little accomplished, and it does nothing for the birds. The guy who always has his television on next door has his television on. Cartoons: bright colors shimmering like an oil spill in a little square. The rest of the landscape is brown and white, wood and snow and house.

I feel like a house today, square and immobilized. There are two abandoned swimming pools. One is mysteriously drained, no matter the season, though I've never caught a glimpse of the drainer. The other fills with leaves and snow, ice and wind. A weather catcher. Today it's filled with snow. A hexagon of white. There must be some safety reason for the hexagon, or more likely, it's pure marketing: Four out of five children prefer their abandoned pools hexagon-shaped. But back to the birds. I'm myopic, so I thought a leaf was being tossed across the pool by the wind, but then I realized that the motion was intentional, birdlike. Bird.

See, I used to dream of alien abduction. Bring on the flashing lights, pointy faces, anal probes! I would signal to them from my parents' roof, hoping they would spot my intent through my Martha Graham arm movements. But now I'm too old. What master race would want a middle-aged specimen with a flabby middle and graying pubic hair? And then there's the dental dilemma. I've had some fifteen thousand dollars' worth of work done on these babies, all of which will decay or worse within the decade. Who is going to fix my cracked fillings, upended root canals, and receding gums when we're on the long journey back to the home planet?

Don't give me that "the aliens will take care of it" routine. The aliens are not your mother. Why would they know anything about dentistry? How do you know they even have teeth? So the only solution is to take a dentist along for the ride. Just picture it: a decade stuck on an alien space vessel, with no one to talk to except your dentist. It defeats the whole purpose of the alien fantasy. If you're going to be stuck with Dr. Dullardstein, you might as well stay on earth. The earth is seven shades of dull today. But it turns the pool water a stunning shade of brown. Brown water. It has unseemly associations, but it's quite beautiful; outdoes blue by leaps and bounds. The birds are an extension of the brown, the air version of the water. I want to hold one, feel all that fluttery life in my hand. Carpe diem, seize the bird. This day sure is a seizure, ma petite mal.

So I know what you're wondering. What the hell does any of this have to do with the bequest? With the revolution, Bhopal, Ian? With Laura Nyro? With capture? With my alarming owlisms? Pink rooms, dental dramas—what the hell?

Well, think of it. Being a revolutionary posed similar dilemmas. What happens when you're on the lam, running away from the sheep, and your crown falls out? The one on that bottom right molar. To admit to the need for dentists seemed hopelessly bourgeois, so I chewed on the left side for a week and ignored the pain spreading from gum to ear.

It was the week that we hid, occupying a small hotel in western Connecticut, waiting to see if our plot to explode Bhopal's detonators would work. Your father was anxious, using his Swiss Army Knife to carve notes on his arm. For a pacifist, albeit a hockey jock of one, he loved blood. Or maybe his pacifist phase—our pacifist phase—was over by then. We just didn't know it.

Sigh. This is getting depressing. We know how it ends: here. A room a toilet. And snow, so much fucking snow.

The snow is everywhere. Thudding along, killing everything, a dogged riot of death and continuance. Trotting on, absolutely miserable and just fine, thanks. What's to be figured out? No matter how hard you try or what you learn, there will be more death, more continuance. And if I were set free, if these bars were melted down into pools of themselves, well, then what? Of course, I'd like to be free of this particular Jerome, but then there's the next. And the next. And more loss, death, continuance. "Loss": a funny word. It implies it could be found. I want to be fixed like any animal. Vet me.

Unpettable, unvettable. Did you know that Shakespeare invented "un-"? Sort of.

How can you "sort of" invent something, right? Well, "un-" was around since about the mid-1500s, but Shakespeare, whoever he was, put it in his plays, in circulation, into common usage. Unuse me.

In much the same fashion, I am sort of an owl. Let's put it in common usage. Try using it every day: sort-of-an-owl it. Which would put me in league with the Bard, eh? Sort of.

Continuance: things go on. There's that barn, its roof visible through this window.

All of it bewilderment, the sensation of watching the white snow on top of the barn roof dissolved into whiter sky. Where is that line?

A sort of habit. A kind of nun.

Thundersnow. Did they have that word back then? Back there. "The '80s." Snow wimple. The past: a planet I keep looking for. That line between roof and sky, then and now. Death and continuance. Not life. What is it? A small itch on my leg about three inches down from my kneecap. A flock of birds gathers on the peek of the roof, forming a straight line. Of bird of line.

Suddenly it's dark. It's been darkening but I haven't been paying attention. Baby, it's outside outside.

This is flat. This is not in flight. And we were.

Birdbomb

Let me start again:

Lovebuzz, love buzz, her head is buzzing with love. She can't look at him, it's like trying (not) to look at the sun, like holding yourself underwater until you have to breathe or burst.

Burst! They're having sex and it's bad. He's decided to chew on her clit like it's a wad of gum can she grind an orgasm out. Nope. The badness of it clings in a cigarette smoky sort of way. It's there, ew yuck, saturating, gross, but it will wash out. She imagines telling him how bad it is, he is. Laura Nyro is warbling on about that flimflam man of hers. It's 5:27 and she needs to pee; should she pee in his mouth? Instead she pulls his head up and flops his cock out of its pouch. Yes, the undies are pink. Men's but pink, magenta actually, did he dye them. No, Caren must've. In a rage she forces him hard, pushes him dry into her no she is not even vaguely aroused. Dry dry dry. The most jealous she's ever been.

She looks up at the ceiling and calls to the seed. It knows how to sow, it says inside her. O possibility—

And then they are not having sex. In fact they are having mac and cheese made from something other than wheat and dairy.

Couscous? Ian has this idea that couscous is a wonderfood, full of vitamins and fiber: practically macrobiotic. So they are eating curried eggs (Cordelia's specialty) and couscous overcooked with margarine and a few inexplicable cubes of Swiss cheese. Sperm racing to the finish line, nerdy little heads packed tight with code. Hurry, boys! Beyond the eggs, Cordelia never cooks. Sometimes she buys them all pizza. She is wishing they had pizza now, mozzarella instead of this gluey Swiss sticking to the roof of her mouth. She forks a clump of it. Semen drips out down her thighs, the odd splotch hitting her bare big toe. Surprise! Couscous is really just pasta, an evil white colonial enterprise. But she doesn't say it. She looks now here levelly at him. "What is the opposite of dreamy, dream-like?"

"Which? They're not the same, Cordy."

She knows they're just eyes, but still. Somewhere in the background a radio shifts between two stations. His stare. She wakes to it a stinging thing the radio shifts back to the moment before she awakened. He is studying her, sitting at the foot of the bed, staring her awake. Even asleep she's mesmerized. Even when he doesn't speak, she hears him:

I will need you to die.

How?

Caren planned it. Maps, charts, backups, escape routes, alibis, the works. And yes, Cordelia's death: that she planned, too. The word was never uttered but. You will detonate here: an X on a map, a chart, a plan.

Ian was media, worked his contacts at the *Globe and Mail*, the *Post*, the *Times*, *The Wall Street Journal*.

Eh? *The Wall Street Journal?* Caren smiled, no teeth.

You can sneer all you like, but when we're on the front page of like every publication in the unfree world, we'll see who's laughing. He makes her face, that sneer, gives her ass a tap, and sticks his tongue straight into her smile; she bites, he squeals, etc. Are we still playing. Che vs. Vlad, cowboys vs. Indians, Patty Hearst vs. that raincoat. An elaborate form of dress-up.

And Cordelia?

Cordelia is to explode.

Cordelia: bird: bomb.

Angel of Bhopal.

Her final flight.

She is therefore absolved of all preparations; better she knows as little as possible, in case . . . (unspeakable: nothing in the neighborhood of "capture" was uttered, not once, not on a dime, okay?). She sees the X on the map and that's it.

You are X.

Silence. It gathers, a thick golden orb of it. Tangible as a halo in a medieval painting, thicker, more solid than the saint herself. An illuminated Cordelia. Such a nun, such a one. As if she's already a martyr—they don't use that word, of course: too religiousy, ick, but that's precisely what she already almost is. Chosen, golden. Almost.

Bhopal was rehearsed, the ever-changing facts knitted, unraveled, embroidered, mass-produced. Invoked like the new Jerusalem, a charred ruin, a relic to be loved.

Ian would begin:

Body count.

US exploitation.

Caren would quickly chime in and eclipse him:

The exporting of environmental disaster.

Worse than nuclear annihilation.

Worse than Three Mile Island.

Worse than Nixon.

Worse than the A-Team.

Worse than the Moral Majority.

Worse than Nancy Reagan.

Nothing's worse than Nancy Reagan.

It's February and Bhopal's already buried. It's yesterday's news, edged out by a Stones reunion, National Dentist's Day, Arab-Israeli something or other. Bhopal the Twice-Annihilated.

But we're going to make them remember. Make them pay. Make the whole system come to a screeching halt. We're bringing the ecowar home, baby! Caren is crowing, Caren is high on revolution. Caren is actually just high: cheap weed from some Mexican dude she might or might not be fucking, who gives a fuck. Apparently pot isn't bourgie when its provenance can be traced to a Mexican dude.

Ian is in Bhopal. Deep in, man. Touching it. The running children. Gas in his black-haired nostrils. He can feel the bottoms of his feet scorched. He's removed his clogs. She is touching her bare feet to his. But he's there.

Let's do it up.

Cordelia spins it into a plush and forceful gold. And bird. Gathering feathers, plucked from an old navy down jacket of Ian's, from a dead pigeon in Albert Campbell Square. Beaks. She draws legions of them, an entire notebook full, no body attached. Just beaks. Another notebook she fills with raptors from every possible angle. **Hawk's view**, she labels one. She is learning bird, hollowing out her bones. To learn it is to be it. To owl. To fly.

Bhopal replaced Ian. Became their leader, their northern light. Mecca of gas, of foreign night, of corpses littering the streets. That phrase: "corpses littering the streets." They used it a lot.

They talked about it obsessively, openly, in diners, in the car listening to Joan Baez (Ian) or Violent Femmes (Caren) or silence. Bhopal Bhopal Bhopal. They each pronounced it differently: Ian flatly Americanizing both syllables into equality, Caren making "-pal" the point of emphasis, giving it a kind of gravitas. A talismanic power. Cordelia stuck strictly to the newscasters' version: BHOpal. Oh, they danced it, loud in the streets, at Café du Roi, in bed.

No secret codes. No CIA paranoia. No cell strategy. There was no outside.

So no outside to fear. Just us, our plan. A blurring. Fused by this fire, this absolute truth. By the deed on the horizon. The hatching. And yeah fucking oh constant fucking so fucking sore. Past sore: bleeding. Delighted. She touches me and he's brilliantly alight. $3 = 1$. I can't describe it, no. Fucked and fused.

That's all.

Okay, one image, since you're begging: Afterward. We're chafed and bloody, bitten, sore so sore, numb. A roadkill feeling.

I think I peed in the bed. It's quiet, a looming sort of silence no one wants to break. Ian takes my hands, both of them, awkwardly since we're both on our backs. And Caren takes his hands, I mean really takes them, grabs them tight.

It seemed bottomless and it was. Even when we weren't fucking we were so **fucked**.

I know, it sounds so culty. "I lost my identity."
No.
There was no losing of this here self, no assiduous washing of brains: I became more me, Caren more she, Ian more Ian, too Ian.

Me entirely myself. Wings folded tight. Claws pulled in. Each in our bodies, our future sarcophagi. Waiting to be split.

The fucking nearly fucking killed us. We were brutal. Every wound opened. To get to that place beyond body, in body. The battleground after the battle.

None II

We are all kinds of nuns. Fresh from the bucket list: Bermuda, Tangier, India, oh there must be loads more. My bucket overfloweth: Bombay Morocco China Fred Astaire . . . what don't I want for Christmas? In prison, we have bucket lists galore. And you a TV ghost. You, who claimed undying love for me in a T-shirt advertising autoparts. To get the Sunday paper on Saturday night: to know the city's disjointed jewels were ours for the buying (ah money, the catch, but let's parenthesize that dirty ditty). To dance, to dream, went the title of my favorite children's book. Did you ever actually *go* to Jake's Bodyshop? Can I flower into a better saint? This is what I wonder as I take your absent hand.

Well, I'm happy to report that we can cross one item off ye olde prison bucket list: Find That Nun. Deep in the bowels of the prison library microfiche, I found her at last. My burning nun. See, Sam: told you so. I knew there was a woman. In the center of Saigon, at the height of the American-Vietnam War, circa 1967. Burned herself to a crisp. Phan Thi Mai was her name, crouched before a white cloth on which she had written, "Virgin Mary and Goddess of Mercy, Help Me to Fulfill My Prayer." An interfaith prayer of peace, the American newspapers called it, without even the faintest whiff of irony. Tonight I crouch before Jerome in homage. I join you, Phan Thi Mai: I say your prayer. I burn.

Oh Jerome. Caren is dead, and Ian is an American policy wonk. Deader still.

XIII

ODE TO IAN

HOW TO GET THERE from this coal lump so petty and concrete?
I want a million bucks a billion I want it all.
Can women have it all?
The question always already answering itself. Ring ring!
Cheers to you, diamond.

Attachment to things, commodity fetishism that soap smelling of melons and more sludgy and true is this lust for people interchangeable lambent humans burned in this genocide. Which is more obscene? This scarily intransigent bottom-of-the-soul need for the druggy power of money its force its shitty things piling up and up or this scalding of bodies. We can all be replaced, the orgasm whispers. In the hotel room you rasped which hole and I was supposed to reply I don't know. But I did.

Somewhere something green. Somewhere in this is the rain damp leaf bare life, cake, something something with flowers.

You are all kinds of nuns tearing dogtuna at my waistless

gait. Night and I love you, your feet, frogs in general, this particular fey. Listless settles and squawks. Night and I eat ravens. This isn't a metaphor. Sigh and love my neck. Stare down this despair bottomless pickled. Will you prance? Lacey. The safe horror of house. I saw my skin: rhetorical, beautiful. Surrendered from my flesh. A devoured thing. Devotion to linen. Lighthouse, darkship, oyster, sailor. Street. Collards and dirt. Prison.

Speaking as ghost, I can't say what fluids feel, what Elmer Fudd felled, or which tuna is chinoiseiest. Apéritif? Ants crawl, buildings sigh, and I am not sure when is the time we'll meet again conjoined, my darling, my Klingon.

Don't mind the above; that's just me in my pink room, memorializing my last night with Ian and Caren. More later, xox-Cordeliaxxx

[prison call]

It was on the day the Pentagon was hit that you called. The Towers didn't surprise me; they'd been hit before. But the Pentagon! It had so bravely resisted the concerted attempts of armies of swamis to levitate it in the '60s. We had thought it too cheesy a target, too obvious, too impenetrable And here it was, all those tetraquadrupillions of tax dollars, blown to hell. And you. In the phone, expecting the machine. But in prison they were ahead of the curve: no machines.

YOU: I'm not calling to talk to you; I just wanted to see if you're okay.

ME: But you are. Talking to me.

YOU: Heh heh. Yes. Okay. So you're okay.

ME: (*I love you*)

ME: Uh. Yeah. I mean, I'm not going anywhere. Ha ha.

[Prison humor vs. gallows humor: Which is unfunnier? Discuss.]

YOU: Um. Okay. 'Bye, Cordelia.

ME: 'Bye, Ian. (*I love you*)

I put the phone down and picked at my salad. Lots of that licorice shit on top. Too much fennel, served up in Aunt Veal's ungainly pottery. Just like home. She'd brought it to me the one time she visited me here, and the guards I guess thought it too ugly to qualify as contraband, so here it was. We had lots of it at home, because every year Aunt Veal would have a dinner party that was really just an attempt to guilt her friends and family into buying some pottery. All my parents' friends had a tureen or two. Veal-ware, we called it. When she and Dick split, there were no more tureens. Women lost whole continents of friends in divorces back then. I wished I had the plant that Veal had potted right into this very tureen, back before she was left Dickless. It lit up, that plant. Like a lamp. I do wish I knew its name. It was something leafy and common, the sort of plant storekeepers like because it's green, a nice lusty verdant hue, and grows like a weed.

Wait, I'm misremembering. The plants didn't light up. No, they turned on the lights! You squeeze a leaf, and a neighboring lamp glows on. Hmm, that doesn't seem so magical. A cheap party trick. I can't find the explanation, despite a hundred failed computer searches, but frankly, the whole thing seems rigged.

Aunt Veal's pottery and the plant lights seemed part of a set. Both of my aunts were crappy crafty: Veal with the clunky pottery, always dripped with orange and white glaze, and Gremlach with the sewing, always skirts, always calico, adorned with her whimsy—yup, she really called it that. "Let me get a little whimsy on this here skirt, honey." Whimsy included buttons, glitter, elastic cloth cut in a wavy pattern, and whatever random flotsam and jetsam the whimsical gods washed up on her sewing box's shore. The skirts were maxis (ankle-length or worse) or minis (crotch grazers). The fabric always patterned, cheap and thin.

Slow, washed-out, denimy. Roll the film of my childhood, anyone's, the '70s, and even their cynicism seems naïve, amateurish. Vietnam? Ha! Just wait 'til Iraq, doll. I put down the phone and forgot you. Blew up my Pentagon and swam into this sort of *Easy Rider* version of my childhood. A film, literally: something congealing over my memory. I was a child and too young to see most of these seminal semeny '70s semi-classics. Yet, still, it's all familiar: the skinny bad-skinned blondes, the guitar- and bike-toting dudes with hurt lines around their eyes and long shaggydog hair. I don't want to go back there, but rather in there, inside that faded mellow yellow landscape. Parse the difference. It'll take you a while. Eons. Don't worry, sweetheart. In here, we have lots of time to stretch and fade.

Need

Prison is a castle built of it. The other thing here is ass. Sitting on it, as in, "You are just an ___," wasting your very life, as Jerome accuses me with his donut face. I a white body amidst the black and brown. Though you'd think from the way this report is going that it's only me and Jerome in here.

No such luck. Girls, lots of them. These girls. Dressed in themselves. Bleach and tweeze and lift. Coated in their skin, prepared for the elements. At mess—yes, they really call it that, truth in advertising, I suppose—I often think of standing up and giving them a proper soliloquy. The world, girls, is as lovely and spent as it ever was. So wrap up tight in your skin. Lie down, and then . . . if I could, I would surely saw me in half.

"Saw": a short active verb loaded with dual action. Cut and see. I saw so much. Some are born great, some achieve greatness, some have greatness thrust upon them. Caren was the reciter, the one to whip out a quote or epigram or even, god forbid, a whole scene from the Bard himself. Oh Caren. This sentence can go anywhere it wants, but I am stuck here, in bed, beside the toilet, behind the bars.

And so are you. Well, you're dead.

Sandwiches for lunch: their last words before they turned the key in the latch.

Twelve Marys hailed by the lady in cell 276 to the left.

Twelve dancing princesses.

The first week I counted the bars. (I would say obsessively, but is it really obsessive to engage in a repetitive activity when deprived of any other stimuli?)

To move or not to move. That wasn't the question in here. I watch my fat accrue like a debt, compound interest around the thighs, yellow blobules multiplying at exponential rates. As with all debt, the fat gained a certain inverse momentum, negative gravitas. I felt a weighted freedom. Nothing to lose but fat and time.

Twig or Wig

The year after capture, that long year before my permanent interment, all I could see in any landscape were nests. I closed my eyes and I still saw them, dense black inkblots stuck to trees. I saw a winter forest flurrying by the train, and catch and hold the nests still against the lines of leafless trees flying by.

Now I see birds. They are harder to catch. Some days, I dream of the bars, the stench of the body and the equally sharp stench of bleach meant to cover it. The lionless sheets. O my Jerome. Wake and sleep bleed into one another, night stepping on the toes of day. I sleep more and better here.

My Jerome, ma petite abeille, ma mère, ma reine. I've never seen you asleep. Sometimes I stare into you in the deep night and see her. Caren? Not exactly.

The thing that immolated her, burned her nun. I see it. Not sex, not revolution: the thing underneath it. Manifest on its surface.

Huh?

Caren's sweater. Her habit. After all, the nun's coating is her core.

A square of light shimmers on the floor, solid and melting at once. A spaceship. Well, it's 5:57 no :58, and my daughter they stole her my lover they killed her and hey I'm [still] alive

Why?

XIV

RAVEL

WHAT I CAN TELL YOU is that one minute I was staring deep into her sweater drawers, noting how perfectly aligned each sweater's edge was with the next, eyes stroking the layers of fabric, feeling the weight of cotton on cashmere on wool, and the next thing we were tearing it all off: sweaters, socks, check-patterned black and purple underwear. I was noticing some orange woven into her turquoise sweater, draped unbuttoned around her shoulders like some expensive college girl in a mail-order catalog. Orange glinting blue. And then I went into an abstract place, of shape and texture and light, not distinct from that thread, dissolving Caren into the detail of the moment. Thread light touch and, and . . .

I mean sex is always like that isn't it tugging us away from time, but what I mean to say here is that I raveled Caren.

Don't worry: sex wasn't the end of my sweater lust. Even (almost) better than fucking was this sort of digressive fondling, neck back and finally breasts, sweater tightly on, sweater fuzzy, alive, a better skin. I still loved the turquoise one the best.

"Wear it. That one." I did it, yes, I told her to wear it—and she did! To the victor go the spoils of sweaters. Yeah, it was the texture, the feel of her under it, knowing I could go in and under now. But also that pigment, so dense. O turquoise night obliterate me.

Last Night

So that was three months ago. And now they're lying in a king-size hotel bed smelling of bleach and feet, ready to blow up the world. Cordelia in the middle. In a panic. Caren is smiling; Ian is blank. Hard. He puts her hand on him, Caren unzips it. Cordelia leans back, ready to be had.

It's just perfume, right? He'd sniff it off of her, nose her clean, breathing in her arms, toes, thighs, ears, nose, and more. Nosing her nose. Doggy dogged. And she'd smile, not answering, trying to look as mysterious as Caren did when asked whether her hair was natural. The trick is not to reply. To radiate, instead. But it was just perfume: Eau Dynamisante, "firmness-freshness-vitality" in a bottle. She'd put on her dark red lipstick, spray three spritzes each behind her ears, wrists, knees, crotch, and suck in her cheeks: her photo face. Smell it. She tried to relax in bed with them, be fully present, alive in her body, in theirs, but it was futile. She couldn't help competing, couldn't shake the feeling that she was the third wheel, the extra tit. Like she and Caren were performing for Ian, fake porno lesbians, even though they regularly and happily fucked each other without him. Somehow it was a show. The turquoise sweater and all it promised, unraveled.

So. What Cordelia really wants now is to have him alone. He has this fold on the side of his face; it isn't a dimple, and doesn't chisel anything. Is it hers. She can touch it now, tomorrow, anytime. Is it hers. Torment of watching it nuzzled by his forefinger.

By Caren's forefinger. No, erase that. Can desire subsume jealousy? Eat it whole.

So it might be the last night of her life, and what is she hoping? To fuck her boyfriend alone. How slutty. How shallow.

[Also delicious]

Her opportunity comes (as it were, har har) when they realize they're out of matches and nobody thought to bring a lighter. Shit, you'd think since we're all failed nonsmokers, someone would have a light, but no. So Caren goes for a Fuckoff-and-matches run, Ian settles on the bed, flipping to the sports channel, and Cordelia is blowing him so deep she might choke might die, makes him come quick and hard, mmmm she swallows it all down. Nothing left. He barely knows what's happening but he does. He manages an exhausted finger fuck. Never one to leave the girl behind, our Ian.

What was that, he smiles into her hair, sniffing her in, this skin. Cordelia gives him Caren's patented mysterious who-knows-if-it's-perfume smile. It has so many uses.

Caren is annoyed when she comes back and smells what's happened. Her tongue notes the dried cum on Cordelia's mouth cheek thigh. Ian is asleep, rosy. Caren drifts herself around him, a sloppy second's sleep.

Leaving Cordelia alone, awake. The racehorses, that's what she calls it. One unbridled thought bolting past the next. Swimming is a right not a privilege. I'm having a constitutional moment under your comforter. Is that trademarked? Women beware women.

She feels doggy dirty and she is. Scummy, literally. It's dried excrementally on her ass, tits, face. The Miracle of Semen: hot and delicious one minute, cold-pizza gross the next. Buried alive, living buried. About to be buried for real. Perhaps. Should she go like this, hair frizzing, clowning around her face, skin dirty with him and her and them? What kind of beautiful corpse will she be. That's not a question, exactly.

Cordelia pulls her scummy body in, fetuses inside the arc of him. Curls her hand around his back, paws his chest: mine. When she first started sleeping with him, she knew Ian had other women. She preferred to keep it vague, abstract. Other. Nameless. (Helen, and Caroline . . .) But she *knew*, biblically, specifically, Ian had Caren. Repeatedly. It was in the room during meetings, during photocopying, during gray vegetarian meals, enduring. She preferred to think of it in some animal category called "just sex," but this was mineral and vegetable, too. He never told her when it started, of course. Didn't need to. He just stopped meeting Caren's eyes, carefully avoided her thumb and index finger when he passed her a sheaf of papers, stopped mentioning Caren's name. Cordelia tried to just file Caren under "other women," blur out the sharp edges, the orange mane and round mouth, but instead she caught it, too, like some teenage outbreak of mono. Cordelia wanted her. Was it her desire or Ian's, she wondered even later, much later. Even now. I mean the turquoise sweater thing certainly seemed hers. But it unraveled.

Now she is in bed with them, in the hotel's squishy queen. The first time it was in Caren's hard twin futon, after a meeting, after a fifth of Fuckoff. Three bodies in a bed made for one. Lean back, Caren whispered, and she did, closing her eyes, opening everything else, letting them in. You are invisible, she told herself, the sour-smelling pillow, the air. It was the only time she wasn't anxious, eager to please, feeling somehow outside it all, even when Ian and Caren worked to make her the center.

Worked hard. O the labor. Caren holding her hands over her head, kissing her throat while Ian pumped away inside her. No, this first time was the best. Let's hold it there. She felt as if she were a bystander, succumbing to the air, even as she held Caren open as Ian entered her, like a doorman, she imagined herself in a uniform: a bow tie.

Then the Dancing

Feet, just feet. Naked, brown, generic. Innumerable toes. Then bodies. In motion, a blur at first, then there's a pattern to it. Abstract, everywhere. Like when you stare at the snow until you are snow. These people are running. These people are dying. These people have feet.

Below herself she's coming, a visible fountain. His grin covered in it. She those feet, moving in some way that involves an immense choreography of repetition. An endless death.

Under Caren. Under Ian. She is an object: an instrument, even, her pleasure a vehicle. A device: a thing to be used. She struggles against the thing preventing her erasure. Even those designed for flight must work hard at it, must flap against gravity.

Everything disappears, zeros and exes and a percussive groan that is her own. O erase me oh. Ian pries her eyes open, Caren touches her eyeballs could this make her come yeah.

A round silence afterward. She feels its curves. Ian flops into sleep. Caren is still touching herself, that thing where she can't stop coming like something slaughtered. Cordelia still a vehicle.

Something soft. A loving slaughter.

Then they're asleep. Now silence.

XV

BHOPAL, CONNECTICUT

AND NOW THE END. Of we three, this world. You are my violet and I am your plum; you are the smart one and I am dum dumb. A private language of glances and giggles. The night we pooped together, child words and all, outside in a field, under a slice of moon ripped from a Moorish flag. Ian watching, teasing, feigning revulsion, Ian the girl here.

Afterward we made Caren break into the church near Café du Roi, a stolid cinderblock affair. She hated it quietly. Constantly. Religiously, yes. All those times it seemed like Caren was retreating into some private Zen palace of stillness, she was actually in her church of church-hatred. Caren hated church, hers but also anyone's, the building and concept, the republic of belief for which it stands, monotheism, under god, indivisible invisible church, with the vehemence only a preacher's daughter could muster. Two of her four brothers were preachers, and the sister was some sort of lady attaché in the same church. What was it like to hate something so passionately, so ruthlessly, so sexily? Of course, it was a form of belief. A form of discipline, a format for her desire. Her god. Cordelia was jealous. Ian was like, well, we're Jews. Doubt is our religion. With a side of pastrami. Oy! The hotel breakfast bacon is wafting in. Time to wake up, pop the pill, and go blow up the world.

Cordelia is on the pill. I mean, everyone is on the pill. Is Caren on the pill? On it, like standing on top of a giant white orb. Cordelia is wedged between them; they are playing sleeping footsie, Caren's toes reaching past hers to Ian's. A flush of rage, disappointment, envy burns her stomach, her cheek. It's confusing. She's familiar with jealousy, the burn of it, this desire to set fire to Caren's red hair, but then she's also the lover of the Other Woman in this particular scenario, in this squishy queen bed. It doesn't cancel out the burn, but dampens it, makes it smolder under the polyester-blend comforter. She pulls a sheet over them. Blue and tan lions loll across these sheets, their legs. His mother's gift. Aw. He brings his bedding with him, even to cheap American hotels. Even to a revolution.

Her mouth is dry, her mouth is theirs. She hates sleeping with anyone, literally sleeping, and now, (possibly) her last night on this earth, she's sleeping with two. Flummoxed and fucked. Cordelia closes her eyes.

This gray dawn speaks:
Have you forgotten flight. Have you no wings.

She is pulled apart, petal by petal, leaving only stem. A bendy thing. It's dark and something is lurking. Hunger. And the thing behind that. She wasn't surprised that Ian wanted to sleep with her; generally, men did. Don't worry—it didn't mean they liked her or anything. She had big tits. She knew he did when they were photocopying posters for the demo long after midnight, and somehow they got into a conversation about desire and revolution and you have big tits, which is like having a big cock. It's power, he said evenly, meeting her eyes as he passed her the stapler, the one that never quite worked. You have to jimmy it, he said just as evenly. Yeah. Only his sly smile belied the other thing. So you want to show me your big cock, she smutted at him the first time, a few weeks later. He didn't remember: Oh yeah, he groaned, pulling it out. Big, as advertised, and was he ever proud. Big tits, she grunted as she pulled them out, knowing he was missing the enormous irony.

She was this: a big-titted mammal. And this, this stupid scenario, the memory of same, is now making her wet at 3:57 the night before she's going to blow them/her/world up? Desire. So pretty, so jealous, grunts the dawn.

Cardrome

Caren doesn't believe in jealousy; Ian doesn't believe in belief. Cordelia isn't sure what these terms mean, the way Caren and Ian push them around. It's like they're playing air hockey, just push push and they ricochet, a kind of weighty nothingness accruing around them.

It's morning. She is in the trunk of a car. She is air. She thinks whenever she gets claustrophobic: we're all just molecules, carbon, hydrogen, oxygen, just like air, we are air, I, Ian. Sometimes it works. A noise: her stomach. Oh yeah, she still has a stomach, so she isn't actually air.

Fuck America. So commands the T-shirt Ian is wearing inside out. He's driving fast, he wants to fuck America, yeah, fuck it up its corporate ass. Fuck it like only the child of a draft-dodger-turned-dentist could fuck it. He loves to hate "it," though she isn't sure what it America is to him. To her it's TV, *Sesame Street*, can you tell me how to get to Disneyland, where her father took her when she was seven. There were long lines but she loved it anyway, getting kitted out in the mouse ears, seeing Cinderella—a real princess!—smoking a cigarette, draped over an older man's arm. America: a cartoon, even as she drives through it, even as she kills it.

Caren has little to say on the subject beyond the usual generic radical rhetoric. The pigs, the dogs, the asshole rats: American beasts.

At the antinukes conference in eleventh grade, Cordelia had first found them: the lefties. She'd also gotten high for the first time, driven home high with someone named Dirk, that's his actual name, she giggled "Dirk" aloud to the car's blue ceiling: So that's why they call it "high," I'm floating, Dirk. Dirk! Kept talking-floating into the next day. And there's a slim, silvery line between that night and this morning, shall she follow it?

You are the oldest you've ever been. Ian is whispering, clasping her hand to his heart thump tha-thump. She's on his knee. Nobody sings. They've stopped so she can barf at the side of the road, carsick, trunksick. So no more trunk. Caren is driving mercilessly fast. Ian is in the back and in the mood. Yeah, well, so are you. So is Margaret Thatcher. So is Bananarama. So is everyone. She half sneers as she says their names this litany. But you most of all, he whispers. His other hand is under her shirt, targeting her nipple. Ouch, and oh, so I'm like a special kind of old? A special kind of young. He's still whispering; it makes her get louder, gain traction, scream. Well, fuck you. And fuck your mother. Fuck your cousin. No, fuck *your* cousin—oh, wait, you already did. Ha ha very funny. In your dreams. In *your* dreams.

Her father is watching somewhere, tracking the rented bronze Corolla as it worms its way through West Hartford.

Ian has both hands under her shirt now, titties, old titties, he cries repulsively. The oldest titties you've ever had. Her father in the hot tub, his hands on her mother's bare small breasts, meeting her eyes. After that who cared. Fuck off, fuckface. She seizes Ian's head and kisses its mouth, all hers. Doc Watson on Caren's cassette player. She feels something large and unruly, a steel wool ball of something scrubbing against her childhood. What is it, nostalgia? No, worse: I wish I were a kid, no be honest: more than wish: won't accept I'm not a child. Does she want to feel this. Yes she does. "Old Groundhog," "Will the Circle Be Unbroken," and her father's favorite, "The Tennessee Stud." She misses him, them, singing loudly without shame. Here comes Sal with a snicker and a grin, groundhog gravy all over his chin.

She climbs on his lap, whispers "Daddy" in his ear, fingers his stubble, puts her finger in his mouth, suck it, he laughs and does, and then it dissolves into sex, flight. All over her chin. Tennessee stud had its Tennessee mare. She's in tears, in love. Ready.

XVI

GAS LUST

SOMEWHERE A CHILD RUNS BAREFOOT. The air is not her friend tonight. The wind tears her eyes, rips her clothes, laughs a methyl isocyanate laugh. Somewhere I am green and safe beneath the earth. Somewhere close an owl hoots, a heart sound, in and out. Will we survive our cruelty. Who will thrive on such cruelty.

Cordelia wakes from her nuclear dream. You know, the one where it's happened. Always it's the mushroom cloud, the fallout. But it turns out it's gas.

India was farther away then. "The third world." There were no Starbucks. Old, crowded, far. Poor, poorer than poor. *Oh! Calcutta!* killed on Broadway, but tanked in Toronto. Mother Teresa, Gandhi, lots of dirty skinny men in rags drifting into the Ganges. Burning bodies, burning wives. Still a favorite pit stop for '60s nostalgics, college kids seeking secondhand enlightenment. How we despised them, their tie-dye colonialism. Fuck that shit. Fuck the queen, castrate her crown. We loved Britain, or at least what we knew of it from the imports: cute accents, ragged sound, the unforgiving mockery. Don't call it "England," Caren instructed: It's the UK. She was performing a little surgery, removing my suburban tropes.

And Bhopal was—where?

The capital of the state of Madhya Pradesh. The capital of nowhere. We'd never heard of Union Carbide either, for that matter. It sure had that Third Reich ring to it. But there it was: front page news, all over the world, even in Toronto, in its provincial *Globe and Mail*: EXPLOSION IN INDIA: GAS LEAK DEVASTATES. The *Times of London*: INDIAN GAS GAFFE RIPS RURAL INDIA. The *Times* could always be counted on for sibilance. A few days later: MOTHER TERESA CARRIES HER MESSAGE TO BHOPAL. Does she now. SPECIAL PRECAU-TION USED IN HANDLING TOXIC GAS, assures the *New York Times* just days later. Right.

Gas. Gas ripping into shanty towns, wild tons of it escaping from December 2 into 3, 1984. Forty tons of lethal gas leaked: no, more than fifty. Make it sixty, seventy-five, one hundred—who knows; Union Carbide kept shoddy records. Tons upon tons of gas. Invisible, odorless. Official death toll: 2,259; 3,387; 4,871. All these weirdly specific numbers are given, then changed the next day. But they're all wrong, obscenely wrong. The newspapers and pundits and historians eventually settle on a nice round number: Another 8,000 will eventually die. In the future.

Which is where I'm chirping from: my future, inside a prison library that is maybe the last library to lack Internet access. I'm digging through the microfiche and here it is, the official tally: 8,000 dead, plus 558,125 injured. A surly, unround number; still no indication of how they arrived at it. Or who "they" are, who cooked up these numbers. Was it the corrupt provincial government of Madhya Pradesh, which allowed Union Carbide to manufacture all that toxic shit in the first place? Or did good ole Union Carbide pull them out of some random rabbit hat with the same profound respect for human life with which it manufactured methyl isocyanate?

Recall: this is before other disasters of larger scale. Pre-Chernobyl, waaaaaay pre-9/11. But long after Hiroshima. A West emboldened by the bomb, the certainty of it, pressed oh pressed upon by Ronnie and Maggie's gnarled trigger fingers. So ready to finger-bang us to oblivion. Post-'Nam, Agent Orange, Watergate. Post-Holocaust, pre-Monicagate. There you go again, Ronnie shakes his finger, relentlessly unironic. An East thoroughly recolonized by not-so-global capital. Capital born and bred in Danbury, Connecticut.

Smack dab in what felt like the endless middle but turned out to be the actual end, whaddya know, Joe, of the Cold War. Landing us squarely here: post-Cold War.

Post-Bhopal. Where we feel safer and scareder. Imprisoned. Not just me, sweetheart babydoll. Jerome.

Buuuuuuuut back to the backroom of Café du Roi, a day or was it two after the explosion, the not with a bang but a wimperness of it growing, gaining traction.

So a US corporation has the arrogance to just plunk its fetid factory down, Ian plunks his finger down on the table to demonstrate, in a crowded city in Bhopal, India (we would never say third-world backwater but of course that's the subtext) and gas the mothers, grannies, children! And their headquarters, the big-boy fat cats suiting it out, man, losing not a wink of sleep over a few thousand dead Indians, yeah their headquarters are right in Danbury, Connecticut.

We're going to bring Bhopal home, baby. Bhopal is coming to Danbury! India: the place Cordelia's father warned her about, like some wayward badboy. India: where the son of someone's brother had gone to "find himself"—such sarcasm in those scare quotes, fingers wiggling derisively by each ear—gotten on a train in Calcutta to see some idiot guru and awakened unable to open his eyes; a goddamn tsetse fly had crawled up and laid its eggs in there and blah blah blah. So he remained blind, unenlightened? she asks. What? Her father is annoyed, erases the question. Ian has the same what? when she asks if anyone has talked to the . . . what are they, Bhopalians? Bhopalese? Bhopalis?

What?

Union Carbide was a mean mother, no sweets for you. She awakens thinking this, and some webby remnants of a dream, her dead mother? Not her real mother, all power suits and no-nonsense flats and always that undertone of I'm disappointed in you, you're not the daughter I was expecting, you squanderer of privilege, you daddy's girl. No sweets for you. "Who says 'sweets' anymore, anyway?" Cordelia's own voice startles her. Yes, I'm awake. I'm talking. Me. Ian rustles the covers, orange and blue fake HoJos, everything a cheap imitation of a chain hotel. Where are the blue and tan lions when you need them? Bunched up at their feet, most likely, soiled beyond recognition. She pulls the orange-trimmed-with-blue sheet over them both, hoping that the morning will reverse, the sun reconsider its rise. Union Carbide, Union Carbide, I can't abide, Union Carbide, her brain insists on chanting. This calms her. She reviews the plan, and its purpose:

It is our job to hold the pigs accountable. Pink and curly-tailed in a TV courtroom she pictures them. Lewd and ludic. She can't stop repeating, pairing, pears and pairs, lewdly lucid, then back to lewd and ludic. Disambiguate, she commands, but the pairing repeating keeps repeating, pairing. This is terror.

The building plan.
How they'll enter.
What they'll do.

Enter at dawn. Drive right into CEO's parking spot—for some reason, they keep it open. Maybe so the middle managers can gawk at their BMWs. How Ian knows this they don't know, but no one asks. He knows. This building and its habits. There is a pause in security; between 4 and 6 a.m., the night guard leaves and the morning guy is always late. Likes his Dunkin' Donuts too much to get there on time. So that's when we pounce. Caren makes a cat move. Very Ann-Margret. Ian loves this, pats her ass, makes his lip Elvis. This is his revolution.

Caren and I will mess shit up so any evidence is buried. Cha-osed away. And then we'll . . . escape. He keeps it vague so if they're captured they can't confess. Caren and he have choreographed their exit meticulously; he assumes Cordelia has figured out her own dance, knows to fly. Don't say the word "capture," he instructs his brain. Keep it vague.

So Cordelia. He locks her in his eyes, voluptuous straitjacket. You're it. You'll explode and whoosh. You.

He touches her shoulders, tracing where wings aren't. She knows. She is the chosen one, the sullen angel, nun of bomb.

Sleep comes back, rescues her. Delay the day!

Drifts into dreams of her mother, seventy-one and pregnant. Seventy-one. She focuses on the number, as if what, if she were seventy it wouldn't be so outlandish? She is in Toronto. The streets are vague, cinematic. Nowhere she or her mother have ever lived but. Her mother is confessional, worried. Blond. Old and pregnant of face. All face. No body.

She awakens with that traveling feeling. Her mother is beautiful, yes the way all mothers are beautiful to their daughters, at least temporarily, but she is also just beautiful. Hitchcock blond, but warmer. Why didn't Cordelia see it? The road is wide, the road is hers, where will the day take her? She'll make him zucchini-corn-mint fritters, she'll tie her hair in a blue ribbon, and off they'll go. Is this fear? His foot inches against hers. Then sex, all three of them.

Caren's hand still cups her breast. Cordelia was surprised by how abstract it was. The three of them. Her fingers spreading Caren, feeling the uncapturable fuck, touching the going in. Someone farted at some point, who, and they all laughed, and everyone came. In Hartford the world is blooming.

As they drive, Cordelia wants. To seize each bloom, digest every petal. She's frantic to imprint each burst of catalpa bud of cherry in some storehouse of body, of memory. To marry it. O violet bundles, O color, O future fruit, won't you be my wife? She laughs. Ian raises an eyebrow, joins his eyes with hers in the car mirror; she shakes her head, no, nothing. Ian and Caren are in the front seats, decrying the lack of Tim Hortons in the States, in this here State of Connecticut, yeah Dunkin' Donuts really doesn't cut it. Debating the numbers of the gassed, the dead, smoking (Caren) and driving (Ian) too fast, invoking Bhopal every other sentence, everything somehow funny. Cordelia is in the back, willing herself into a plum bud. Or at least its husband.

There's an anxiety to her ardor. Will she love this beauty, will she love it enough, will she perceive this leaf that petal such pink, see it so fully that, what? So she captures it before she's gone. But she'll be gone. And it, the perceived thing, well, the perception if not the thing itself oh god so fucking philosophical are we now: gone. Lush leaves, bloated blooms—all past, in the past, almost (or actually?) before they're fully imprinted, guzzled down by her thirsty synapses, terrified that this beauty will be irretrievable. She won't say the word "dead," but she does rather sternly say this may be your last leaf, final frond, penultimate plum blossom. The sibilance calms her. As if she could absorb it fully enough for the memory to persist beyond life, beyond her. It might outlive her, you know. That plum blossom. And her memory of it.

The front seat conversation shifts: strategy. "So the key is speed." Ian is high on the adventure of it all. "Well, if the left lower entrance is unguarded, we'll have like three extra minutes. Can't count on that, can't count on anything but the pigs. The fucking pigs and their fucking gas. Speed, man." He smiles, enjoying his '60s slang, the flowers disappearing behind the bronze Corolla.

XVII

DANBURY DENOUEMENT

THIS IS HOW WE DID IT:

The shredder, the paper, the pens, the Wite-Out, the spray cans full of toxic shit to clear the gummy shit off your screens, the coffee grinds in big white waffle filters. All nest.

Nest inside of nest: bury it in a chair, bury the chairs inside the desks, bury the desks inside the halls, cars. Vroom. Shred the gray polyester floor, it's already starting in that corner there. Shred the secretary's magnet: *Smile, it's only Monday once a week!* Cordelia frowns as she shreds it all down to a metallic fluff.

She opens one desk drawer, another, all: a desk drawer rampage. Oh, that paper looks promising. Officious, medical. "No signs of HPV or other gynecological conditions." She crumbles into the very center of the nest. Well, don't look a good Pap smear in the mouth. And nibbles. Good voodoo, vajayjay doodoo.

There are so many elegies to look forward to. Stem by stem. She chooses a desk at random: it's a woman's. There's nail polish remover, too many family photos of gap-toothed little boys, and yes: a single tampon readied for an "emergency" in the top drawer. Also a change of shoes: sneakers, pink. Cordelia tilts the desk, heavy, ugh, so that it all crashes to the floor. Done.

Let's go, she tells Caren, Ian, lying post-coital on the boss's bigboy desk. She is the commander now.

Um, Cordelia? How about—(he gestures to her pinks). The explosives, embedded petals in her skirt. The ultimate pedal pushers. I mean that's what we're here for, babe. Are you chickening?

NO.

Where does the finality in her voice come from? Certainty, absolute cruelty. Absolute rule.

I am your queen. I am the hallmark of this transformation. Fall into bird. Fly.

She leads them to the window. She instructs; they listen. We are not to die. We are not to blow it up. We are flight. Be wingéd. Be in sync with light. Be petal and bud. Go.

And they do.

The ledge is pink granite. Orange really, but it's called pink. It's a decade before everyone will make kitchens out of it.

NOW into bird. And flight. Follow.

Cordelia first. Her arms wing, she floats, she flies, she is lighter and pinker than petal.

Then Ian jumps. If he's going to do it, well, he's going to fucking do it up. He wobbles a bit in the air, then it's a straight flight down.

Soft landing. Featherless beast.

Then Caren, debating, deciding, hesitating, the princess of prevarication.

[Explosion, pink.]

For a moment, a long and unwieldy one, Cordelia longs for the bronze Corolla, O to be in the embrace of the way back, surrounded by the safety of mustard-stained pleather. O to be that getaway girl.

Bereft: Q&A

And now I am alone. Without even one lover, much less two. No one but a toilet to talk to.

Q: There must be others. Women not toilets. At lunch, in the rec room.

A: At lunch, in the rec room.
Talking, always talking. Unflushable.
Talking about what women talk about.
Their men. Their kids. Gluten.
Does it make you fat.
In prison just like out.

I told them: Honey, I am not spending the rest of my eternal infernal internment listening to you discuss who or what you put in your mouth. My god. So I chose here. Jerome. Solitary confinement. Immolation, then isolation, hah! Which gun.

Yes, you can choose your method. Shut your flushing mouth. Sorrow my fingers, one by one, pinky to thumb. Sigh, start again.

Parallel Parking

Ian has done his research. He's a huge architecture geek, loves steel and cement, blueprints, models, gets a bit gleeful anytime he sees any skyscraper. Balustrade, quoin, ziggurat. He chews hard on these words he could never spell. A few trips to the public library later and he's got a pile of paper on UNION CARBIDE—

HEADQUARTERS DESIGN. It was a big project, a model corporate office for a model corporate citizen. Launched in '80 to launch the '80s. The papers form a sort of Leaning Tower of Carbide on his desk. He loves to finger them, quote them, delight in their designs. They did like a ton of market research to find out what the corporate fucks wanted. Ah, the yearnings of the yahoos. The chrome-and-steel dreams of middle managers, aspiring coffee-achievers all. He's bleating the details. Ergonomic chairs! Wall-to-wall windows! And—get this—"nonhierarchical work space." It's all in this. He smacks both their butts with a blue-covered report. Cordelia imagines it leaving a blue stain on her ass. Another edifice.

Q: So how did the Carbide carbuncles designing this palace of equality interpret the notion of nonhierarchy?

A: Parking. They made parking lots for each fucking floor. So Middle Manager 37 can drive up to his cubicle, just exactly like Middle Manager 38. So you can drive right up to your prison cell, er, office suite. So you are free and equal to all your cellmates. I mean coworkers.

Or rather, your car is equal, Caren adds. Automotive equality for all autos! They one-up each other: freedom to park. Gas guzzlers unite to take back the right . . . to park! We put the parallel back in parking! Oh, they have fun with that one.

It drifts into a game of unlikely associations. Whoever's is the unlikeliest wins. Wins what? Caren winks: You'll find out.

Cauliflower blossoms: cleavage.

Montgomery Clift: Maldavian sea salt on a fine-boned platter.

Nectarines: a sofa made of well-oiled sardines.

McNuggets: McNuggets. At their McNuggetiest.

Cordelia will not get an "A" for participation, now will she.

She's too tired, too anxious. Too fucked. Her face blank, mouth raw as her recently reamed ass, and bearing the same characteristic royal flatness. So she roils and rolls as they inch toward Danbury, Connecticut, population 57,684. The radio blares, the radio quiets.

Cordelia is composing funeral notes. Elegies for everyone. For Ian, for Caren, for her very dead father. For herself. She's perfected the genre. Open with an idiosyncrasy, the uncommon quirk. Add an anecdote—make it short—revealing a fable/foible unknown to anyone except the recounter. (It's best if it's entirely fabricated.) Finish with a truism that confirms both what everyone knows of this person and the speaker's special knowledge, her privileged relationship with the dead. With all the dead. Each petal.

39 OLD RIDGEBURY ROAD. Not to be confused with New Ridgebury. Very high-class, these murderers. Old money. Hahvahd. Here's the turnoff.

Ian's is easy. Hockey for the opener. An utterly fictional anecdote about his love of the game, his mastery (despite the dyslexia, which he would hate being mentioned, but hey in this scenario he's dead, he doesn't get a vote), no, make that his *incredible* mastery of teams, positions, scores, players, ranks. Oh yeah, she's got it: "A revolutionary who wielded a hockey stick instead of a gun." His mother would love that. Well, not the revolutionary part, but anyway. Next we get the private Ian, the time he cried in her arms over a sick puppy. And yes, she'll mention said sick puppy's name: Bitch. It would add just the right soupçon of reality to Fictional Ian. She is practically licking her chops. How he'd hate the hockey/puppy theme. His bourgie-boy habits overwhelming his revolutionary acts. Well, death exposes us. There is no privacy in the coffin. All his bitches were adults.

Caren, now Caren would of course have the largest crowd.
A popular poppet is she. Her Québécois family would turn out
in force, insisting on a fundamentalist funeral, ministers and
their misses overrunning the show. Cordelia would be a minor
player, her elegy squished between two garrulous cousins who
barely knew her, yet ramble on about their frolicsome Frenchish
childhood in broken-to-the point-of-shattered English. Cordelia
would ennoble Caren, burnish her in a soft orange light visible
even to the most Catholic of cousins. Caren cared for the poor,
the oppressed, the marginalized. Though she was not religious,
she was much like Mother Teresa, who said, "We ourselves feel
that what we are doing is just a drop in the ocean. But the ocean
would be less because of that missing drop." Caren, today the
ocean is missing far more than just one drop. Not a single eye
will remain dropless after that one. Oh, whoa, do it in French.
Baisse manquant: not a dropless oeil in the house after that one,
man. Should she work the sweaters in somehow? Nah, smells too
sexy. But add that anecdote about staying up all Christmas Eve
making bouillabaisse for Saint Barthelme's soup kitchen, yes, pull
those Christian heart strings (leave out that bit about the ménage
she and Caren were conducting on said hallowed eve with Père
Jean Claude, eh).

Her father:
Dead already.
She sees his face, first animated, mustachioed, young, then
bald and dead whoosh erase erase.

Next?

Now there's a wanker of a question: What would I say at my
funeral? To the aunties Veal and Gremlach, over their clamorous

tears, their well-rehearsed performance of sorrow. To Ian. To Caren. To my dearest deadest dad. To my ghost mother. To my corpse. Salut!

There's okay a huge sinkhole Grand Canyon Taj Mahal-minus-the-sublime **splendor** opening under me. It's all very passive, this enormous disaster happening beneath me, to me. Without me. So big too big I can't see it. And am, hmm, yup: sunk by it, the boundaries between it and me blurred. Sunk. Cordelia shrinks into the car seat, eyes closing.

Wake up, girls. We're here. Time to—
(Caren is quick on the draw) Fuck.

Stroke

They are both petting Caren's hair, like she's some exotic orange kitten. Cordelia thinks of her dead mother, her dead mother's love of Russian blues, Persian longhairs, and above all the margay, half-beast half-pet. She'd put bookmarkers in the cat-fancying mags on the pages she liked, and Cordelia would study them, scowling in imitation, hoping to turn herself into a kitty centerfold. Caren would make a great margay, the spectacle of her wildness half her charm. Combing her is so calming, but maybe not for Caren. Ian's eyes are closed, bliss, transported somewhere else but also intensely right here, in her hair. Ian the Caren-fancier.

Cordelia squelches a giggle. And pulls one tightly wound red and gold curl straight, too straight, ouch. Ian does the same, ouch ouch. We are such pigs, Cordelia thinks, and wonders if she's said it aloud, but she scans their faces, Caren's closed eyes, Ian's sly smile as he pulls again, and no. Something is still all hers.

Afterward she curls up away from them, returns her limbs to herself. I smell like them. She sniffs her own hair, gives the thought some teeth. Her mouth, her teeth: coated with them. They are asleep in each other. Unguarded. Ian on his back, his neck at an odd angle, exposed, cuttable. Caren facedown in the crook of his arm, a mass of pulled curls, spent girl. And I? Apart. Unharmed. Unharmable. This is a fiction: I smell of them. In me on me.

Post-carfuck, Caren awakens, prevaricating. "I'm not ready; let's get eggs. Food. Last supper-breakfast."

Days Before. Maybe Weeks.

There was always a pause after we entered the diner and found our table, a moment of suspense before we silently arranged which two faced which one. Caren would clutch my hand under the table when I ended up facing them. I'd feel my hand lose itself in hers. A phantom limb, not mine. Hers? No one's. It was a rarity for Caren to be in this position, for her to face us, me and Ian, and I proffered nothing.

Steve is lying on her bed, rolling cigarettes from a loud orange leather pouch, where on earth did he get it? "Smoking reminds me of how, no matter what I think, say, or do, I'm still implicated in the military-industrial complex." He exhales all over her squat room. A short square of space. The bed dominates.

"Yeah, right. I think you just love smoking." My outlier, she thinks. He's one of them, in the heart of the group, as committed to the always-nebulous Great Commie Cause as any of them, but also not. Apart. Well, he's a musician. A hustler? Possibly. Gay: definitely. She's tried. She's not sure why he's chosen to like her, but she basks in him, his smoke, his bullshit. Of course, the fact that he clearly hates Ian but never says as much, and is indifferent to Caren and her copper beauty, doesn't hurt. She admires the way he whistles Nina Simone during meetings, stays aloof and apart from the internecine warfare. Smokes and whistles, sometimes at the same time. He's the only musician in their group who isn't just a low-rent Dylan imitator, who actually said, "I'll take Bowie over Dylan any day. And I mean *take* him, honey!" winking a blue eye her way as Ian strummed and hummed "Blowin' in the Wind" slightly off-key for the hundredth time. How many times, indeed.

At first she'd assumed Steve wanted to fuck her, the gay thing notwithstanding, assumed his singling her out, wink wink, was only the usual cheap indication of the desire for a quick drunken fuck, but then one night, the night after Bhopal, when they were well past drunk, they took a chaste bath together and just talked, music art religion bands politics big and small and more music, and fell asleep without realizing it, waking up when Ian walked in, smirking. He still didn't believe they hadn't. Just as well. Now they always bathe together.

She shakes her head. I love you, so deeply and purely. Does he hear this.

"So god, Cordy, you've cut your hair like hers now. And that's got to be her sweater. Who else has gray cashmere? What's next—are you going to start talking all BC Valley Girl like her?" He fakes a British Columbian oh-my-gosh-like-really twang, with that provincial soda-gone-flat affect, not Caren's at all.

"I thought you'd be into it, being a giant homo and all. And she's not from BC, pas de tout. Purement Québécois."

"A frog, eh? C't'au boutte." He throws her a towel—Ian's, pink—and smirks. "Well, speaking of giant homos, or giant closet cases, actually. . ."

Ian a homo: What a thought, man. Cordelia laughs and takes off her sweater, leotard, underwear. She unwraps out of the Indian print wrap skirt, Ian's favorite one, with black and red arabesques on a tan background, and pulls the towel around herself. She can't help trying to smell him on it. "Ian is secure enough in his masculinity to embrace his feminine side." She recites Ian's own words as she pulls off the towel and throws it to a naked Steve. His dick is curved, quiet. A fancy friend.

He giggles and makes a Hollywood scarf out of it. "'Secure in his masculinity': oh man. Did he actually say that? God you've got great tits, Cordelia. I hope they appreciate them."

I can't remember what happened next. One moment impales you, the next vanishes.

Should she have run with Steve? Will she die with unappreciated tits? She leans deep into the backseat, wondering.

Caren is one of the world's true beauties, Ian tells Cordelia conspiratorially. What a phrase. Cordelia looks in the rearview mirror, considers her own above-average—hardly world-acclaim-worthy—looks, her large features too indelicate to win such extravagant praise. Her mother was another one of those true beauties the world so prizes: a pouty blonde, black-eyed and high-cheeked. But she, well, she is a smudgy photocopy of her mother: the eyebrows heavier, the jawline squarer. Same features but everything larger, coarser, darker. Her mother, colored in by her father. Attractive, they mutter, striking even, what with the black wiry mane and hazel eyes, but beautiful? No. Nothing to world-acclaim here, folks. Only her mouth is the sort of note-worthy distraction on par (perhaps) with Caren. What man can help imagining its thick purplish lips upon him, what man cannot think of those other lips . . . a dirty mouth for a dirty mind, Ian likes to tell her as he fucks it. Dirty dirty.

She has studied her own face. Studied it like there's an exam: she'd better know it well. She knows it so well. What a delight to forget about it, the curved hook of nose, the exact aperture of eyelid, the fleshy fucky mouth, the too-wide jaw—what a joy to stop this project, this invincible subject: her face. And no, she doesn't replace it with Caren's, with Ian's. She is a student of nobody. Occasionally she will be swept up by his pink mouth, out to sea on the curve of Caren's cheeks, heaven of bones. Sure, she's absorbed. In sex, there, too, are moments of observational beauty. The mottled pink of that nipple. But it is unstudied.

Now when she thinks of her own face, it is an abstraction: my face. Anyone's face. Who cares?

Ah, to have such a face. Caren enters any room and every man, every woman, even the children, gaze upon it, applaud such a glory of creation. One of the world's beautiful women, Ian does not need to intone, touching here now for the last time Caren's so sculptural cheek. You bitch, you sexy sexy bitch, he groans and shoves himself inside Cordelia. There is something to invisibility. To camouflage. To disappearing beside one of the world's great beauties. To attracting nothing, no one. Even Ian doesn't quite see her, just a mirror of his own lust oh god your mouth.

After, Cordelia feels freer, lighter. A plain ghost, happily erasing itself from the visible world. Let's go. The carfuck, the diner: done. Check. Let's blow. It. UP!

XVIII

BIRTHDAY

WOKE IN LIGHT. A dusty sea of it. A window, barred. Outside flatlands. Lawn, no hills. Is this Connecticut. Is this a cell. Awake and there are many bulbs, fluorescent. Peach walls—a feminine touch? So little to touch, to feel. Linoleum. Grapenuts cereal and milk. A child's breakfast. Will they bury me. Will they grow my bones. O daughters of trickle-down pediatrics.

Outside everything harmonizes, trees and sky and air play their parts. My nose swells and considers this and other things.

The door opens, the light brightens, the plot thickens:

Congratulations! You're pregnant.

Bathed in stun. You sit up. You lab rat: you don't even have control of your own blood. They could take it all. Test it all. They did.

Verdict: Anemic.

And pregnant. Yes, you can get pregnant on the pill. (Actual failure rate: 8%. Didn't your mother teach you anything?)

Lots of red meat on the tray. It's slotted in, on the ground. A makeshift pet door. Nobody enters. And of course, the obvious corollary: nobody exits. So if I were nobody, I could both enter and exit.

This is what your mind does when you're nobody. When nobody comes or leaves for what was it, weeks? Months. A lifetime and then some. There's a toilet. There's the slot. There's the bed. The window. My knees. I take an inventory. I'm bruised on my back, tailbone, knees—hard landing!—and am sleeping off some never-to-be-identified drug cocktail, but nothing is broken. Hands off the merchandise. It's hard to know who to blame.

The window is too high to climb to. It shows sky, a little square of it. Weather and time are out there; in here, they never turn off the light. I train myself to look to the square of window when I wake up in the night, to determine if I should go back to sleep or awaken, though for what? I've rehearsed several plays. Sung an oratorio. Screamed, even, cried for help. Yelled after the mysterious slot pushers. They must collect the trays when I sleep; I caught them once, a hulking male figure in an orderly's greens. Something stuck into me and I was out cold. I didn't try at night after that, but by day, I'd bark and yell. Barking: I'd always wanted to give it a try, though I've no patience for dogs and their smelly ways. I've experimented with hungry barks, lonely barks, sad barks, bad dog barks. Growls from ecstatic to impaled.

One wants to be watched. To be observed. For one's barks and bruises to be noted. Am I here.

Retardation and castration: the twin fates of pets. Ambered in infancy, frozen in your love. Survival of the cutest: the environment, the food chain, the whole fucking earth, basically held hostage to human notions of what's most attractive in an infant. Dependency, round features. A propensity to pee on the couch. I am

pregnant.

A pregnancy is something one is. One is had by it. It contains you, I. She does not feel doubled. Blackout. She thinks of the zucchini pancakes she won't make. Rehearses the recipe: zucchini, duh, feta, lots of mint, wild dill, one egg plus an extra yoke, flour, just a handful—her hand clenches automatically, zombie chef. Mix loosely, casually. Don't beat.

& birth.

This room is bluer. With a green tinge. I guess it's gray, but colorful, like scrub pines. A wealth of tones but all gray, gray scale they called it in art class, but that doesn't feel right at all. A rainbow of grays. The wall is mesmerizing her, hypnotizing away her pain. You are getting not sleepy but painless, you are getting gray, you are—the pain is overtaking, a cell to which she is attached, gray won't do it: green, that late August last green before fall, before change, before birth. My piehole is open. O fill me with grays.

The greasy sameness of prison days now ends.

No rising sun, no lunch, no showers and soiled shirts. No lukewarm water dripping down your chin, contaminating your blouse, as you wash it. No wash. Just Jerome.

In pain. Is pain. Shimmering out from womb to pore. Objective, distant: in a box, placed at a distance. Is pain, she is, pain = she = pain, and she utterly controls it. Her. Pain. Birth is unlike everything.

Everything one cell. Not even pain, for pain is something separate. Everything one, everything splitting open. Body doing things, racing ahead of her. Push they say, and it isn't pushing but exactly the same muscles, the same motion as coming, tighteningreleasing without intent, without purpose. She laughs, why don't they tell you that? Keep breathing, but this assumes volition, control hers to seize, hers to let go, hers to breathe. Her body one cell of pain joy birth. Fearless, for fear involves choice, what will I do ifs, and here there is no such thing. What a relief. What joy, what agony, though the root is "agon," struggle, and there is none, her body its own mind. She remembers the cockatiels of Australia, shrieking wild against the cliffs, common as jaybirds and just as loud. You've already crowned, relax, breathe, it's coming out, no matter what now. She barks.

Her crowning glory. Heir apparent. Bald, actually. Hairless heir here between my legs, is my legs, cunt, whole. Bark, bark. Flies out, whoosh unstoppable

& is born.

A bloody mess. Screaming, that's good, the nurse says, Cordelia hardly notices her, and here's the placenta, good, as unnoticeable as the nurse. O daughters of ergonomics and iced hazelnuts. You have been rent. Pay it now.

And the she of me, I, us was born. Imprisoned. A body. Hers. Still part-mine. Motherfucking motherchild: two.

& was stolen.

XIX

BOMB [REPLAY]

SHE IS MOBILE, a machine for flight disassembled on the gray carpet, witnessed by the burgundy walls, by the "art."

The calamitous O'Keeffe, Caren instantly christened it,
framed in pink. The light tan leather couches, expensive yet
somehow plasticy looking. A black metal coat hanger alone in a
coat closet. Each ordinary office object hateful somehow. Mats
by each door, why? Oh—an unanticipated consequence of that
egalitarian drive-in parking: mud tracked from suburban yards,
foot aromas wafting in from the great indoors straight into the
office with no liminal vestibule, no foyer or threshold to cross.
No outside; a continuous corporate flow. You're in your house, in
your car, in your office. Please wipe accordingly.

"Let's go powder our nose." Caren makes the powdering
gesture on her nose. Cordelia twitches hers sympathetically: our
nose, singular, but doesn't move from her spot on the tan leather
couch beneath the calamitous O'Keeffe. Ian is systematically

unwiring all the wiring, pulling plugs, cutting cords, killing the juice on the many large computers, phones, printers, coffeemakers, staff refrigerator. Just in case. Then he turns to the corner office—yes it's literally in the corner.

"This must be where the big boys underfund Bhopal," he pronounces with a certain formality, and Cordelia and Caren follow him in, as Caren grabs her hand and surreptitiously whispers "Underfund? Try gas." Ian hears nothing.

"Let's see what Mr. Bigboy is hiding." He riffles through the CEO's desk drawers, tossing all the big boy's random shit on the floor. There's a mini-US flag propped on the desk between two generic family photos, the kind they put in empty frames in stores, idealized blondes in mom coats with overdressed kids. Who even wears Mary Janes anymore? And those weird eyelet socks. Ian plucks the flag.

"Come here, ladies. It's time to pledge allegiance."

Caren laughs, salutes Sieg Heil, and puts her hand over her heart.

"I pledge allegiance to the fucking flag of the seditious saints of Amerikkka."

He always writes it like that: Amerikkka. Cordelia knows it's a Klan reference, she gets it, but thinks of it as his stutter, which he confessed to her one night not long after they first met: the childhood stutter, his dyslexia. Sieg He-he-heil.

"And to the Republicans whose testicles stand . . . " Caren grabs his balls, and before Cordelia quite realizes it, they're fucking, hard, as hard as he can, which she knows from experience is mercilessly wonderfully hard, all over Mr. Bigboy's desk, pulling out to cum all over the standard-issue family photos. Caren is touching herself theatrically, making sure there's maximum viewing possible, stretching herself wide, gaping toward Cordelia, but Cordelia shakes her head, no thanks.

Ian kisses Caren, then Cordelia. "I think we're done here. Au revoir, Monsieur Bigboy." Caren takes a piss on his big leather chair for good measure.

Cordelia sits in the center of the chaos, the rubble, broken vases, O'Keeffe shards, shredded paper.

Detonate?

Ian starts it as a command, but by the time he gets to the "—ate," it's a question. They are both staring at her, naked, cum-smeared, flightless.

"No. This is better." She gestures to the ledge, indicates flight. Aviation, not detonation.

And they nod, in tandem.

She nods back: yes.

O bombless flock. This scene will repeat a thousand times in her head. What happened?

The sudden and absolute certainty that she must cancel the grand plan, turn bomb to bird. She pauses on the window ledge, surveying the chaos. This is her throne: semen, woodpulp, glass, wires, Post-its, urine. Her artificial kingdom. There's a chirping sound outside. The catalpas are at full bloom. Past. What is the word for after-bloom? Before decay. Fecund is the quality, overripe is too negative, but what is the verb, the act, what it does before it dies?

Nunstill

The wastebasket: a gold star for good behavior. It was decades before they let me have one, despite it appearing annually on my Inmate Christmas Wish List. It's a risky item; somehow it figures in suicide. But I'm not interested in that form of flight. Still no overhead light; just the natural glare dripping in from outside. But O my basket. It's large, industrial, verging on trash-can status. I nest inside it. I am a particularly glamorous form of garbage. The state's mascot. Its performing bear. Your favorite son, your treasure, quel jewel. A solitaire. Is a zoo animal a pet, and if so, whose? Not the zookeeper's. The viewing public's? Too amorphous. Belonging depends on specificity for its force. See: **I belong to you**.

But there is no public here. Just Jerome. And now this bas-ket.

And you?

I'm yours. Your pet, your prisoner.

And you, well, you are dead. At least there's that. At least you don't have to fucking roll over. If you are Caren, that is. They caught you and killed you.

There was no shootout; only a quiet capture in a suburban diner. Oh shit, I said. I saw them first, their guns smiling out of their holsters. Caren bolted: Caren was shot. I have to repeat it to know it. Caren was shot. Dead.

Caren.

I'm trying to conjure you, call you, ghost you back to bed. Breathe some life into your crumpled lungs.

They shot you in the chest.
Your red hair in a pool of red blood.
Red hair is really just orange. I saw.

But I see nothing. Ghost nothing. An empty shell, an un-developed character. You're a missing person. Well, Caren, you were never much of a person, really. Clothed in rapture, in sweaters, in revolution. In Ian. We together a disintegrated object. An unraveling. Yes I fucked you, was fucked by you, oh gee golly fuck I tasted you in all my mouths. But you, you were not really my lover, **mine**. These sweaters. Taste all my mouths. Ew that's kind of gross and we weren't. Weren't anything. Unfigurable in the landscape of Lenin. Of revolution now! The people united shall never be defeated, lesbian-feminism, macrobiotic couscous. Uncaptured even here. Our nothing our glory. Unthings out of no time. Not even ghost. Oh Caren. I made a thing of you and unraveled it. The more we fucked, the farther from me you were. I saw you die.

So, bye!

If you are Ian, well, that's a birdy of another feather. You slumped beneath the diner table, dragged me down. There was a crumpled napkin, a French fry. Generations of gum. Still life.

Then capture.

Separated, incarcerated.

Dead to each other.

But that's not the end of you, Ian. So: your father engineered an extraction far bloodier than the deepest root canal. Did it up, he did. Flew you back to the American nest. And so you live, a graying parrot. Advocate. For health care reform, unionization, universal dentistry. Advocate! Now that's a word we would have gotten a good laugh out of back in the days of Café du Roi. Beyond bourgie. A lib! Abandoning your stolen child. Allowing the state to steal her away from us. Your terrible theft.

And I left to rot. Swollen. Stolen. Impregnated.

They stole her. Stolen: no synonym. Did they tell you. Did you know. Is she dead, is she with you oh it's overtaking me I can't—

Night, fear. What's the difference. Devouring myself, pancreas by liver.

Okay, get a grip. Name it. Say it: I am terribly afraid of _____.

Everything.

What if this extravagant sacrifice, so rich I think of it as plummy, a wine-describing word far removed from the actual fruit, was for nothing. If Caren died for nothing. If my child were **stolen** for nothing. If I am nothing.

Well.

What have we learned, kids?

XX

WE WERE RIGHT

DON'T LAUGH. I'm already crumpled in a wastebasket. A wastebasket that I had to work hard to earn. How much more degraded can one owl get?

Hear me out:

See, we were absolutely correct, both in concept and method. Absolute in our correctness; correct in our youthful absoluteness.

The enemy is not the state. The state is just another idiot running around half-blind at dusk. A powerful idiot. Too powerful to explode his enemies, or they'll explode him right back. Balance of power, capisce? Fishy, but true.

But these corporations, these fartholes, plundering and leaving, passing the buck. Gas the perfect metaphor for their invisible stinky force, transcending borders and boundaries, space and time.

Except it's not a metaphor. They gassed a continent. Slime merchants. Windbags. Owning the wind itself. Wafting across borders, bodies.

A child runs in the night, the wind breezing poison through her every pore. Corporation: the body made market. The true enemy of the people. Right, folks? I scratch my ass extravagantly, the gesture could take all day. There is no audience here. Plumb me. Come on, try.

O gas, you are neither solid nor liquid. You transform from solid to gas to death. Still the burning nuns.

And me? Oh Jerome, don't you worry your pretty little lid.

I'm not dead. Only molted. Listless, encaged. Window gazing. Today we watched my shadow. O my inhuman life. The most coveted pet is the wildest. Tiger, lion, shark. Noli me tangere! Unpettable, unvettable. You said that night before we burned for Bhopal you wanted me but only for fucking, no talking. No politics. Shhhh . . . Forget Bhopal, forget good ole Union C. Forget Caren. Your legs furring across me, one arm putting mine to sleep. O airless embrace. I was coming home to a room I didn't know was mine. *I am sex for you but what are you for me?* I wrote that night, but really didn't care. I am sex for you, for you! was the important part of that thought.

Here I so horribly am. My room lost.

But not dead. Could we develop the wrist facility, the opposable thumbs, the understanding of our situation to open our cages. Open, and leave. Prisoner and guard alike. And yes, toilet, too. Strolling out, into _____?

Night, fear. What's the difference. Devouring myself, pancreas by liver. Okay, get a grip. Say it: I am terribly afraid of _____.

XXI

BEQUESTED

AND THE BEQUEST TO YOU, my stolen daughter, my codfish:

I. Your mother. Skinned. Her body emptied out, naked, alive. Picture it there, scooped out like a pumpkin. How you first knew it, for you were what was scooped.

II. Iraq Wars, I, II, and now III. More sequels than *The Godfather*. Afghanistan, Afghanistanagain! BP oil spill. Watch those cute little birds getting the black oil washed off them. Chernobyl, duh. Gaza in flames. Gaza again, faster and furiouser, on July 8, twentyteensomething. Soon we'll forget that date just like we forgot Bhopal.

III. Oh, this is so motherfucking political. Look at any dead sea. Watch everything get deader.

IV. The ballet master throwing a slipper at my left tit. In all the years I've been remembering that moment, I've never figured out whose slipper it was. What nun. These cinders.

V. Well, Bhopal. Two generations hence and the place is a fucking disaster. Everything contaminated, everyone mutated. Union Carbide deader than Caren: whored itself out on the cheap to Dow Chemical. Can't be prosecuted, can't even be fined. Ça n'existe pas. No I'm not shitting you: Look it up. Go ahead, really. You're free.

VI. Flight. Specifically, that of Caren's cat.
Let me let the cat out of the bag:

VII. I let the cat out. My last Canadian act, the morning we left for Connecticut. Caren was already in the car, examining her eyes in the mirror. Lifting, lowering those famous brows. Ian at the wheel, scrutinizing the map. Come on, Cordy; let's do it up.

VIII. Free Veal! I gave the Black Power salute in solidarity. She ran out the door, into the alley, a slight grin on her calico maw.

IX. A father and a daughter, locked in prison. Chirpless.

X. Q: What's the missing link?

XI. A: Mother.

XII. This cage. Your touch. Flush.

The End

ACKNOWLEDGMENTS

SARAH SOHN AND NADIA SOHN FINK: my family, my love. Nothing good in my life would exist without you. Including this book.

Thanks to everyone at FC2, especially Lance Olsen, and everyone at the University of Alabama Press, especially Dan Waterman. A million thanks to Amanda Annis, my incredible agent at Trident Media, who believed in *Bhopal Dance* from the start.

Laurie Milner helped Toronto it up with her expert Canadian editorial eye. Thanks also to Rachel Salgado for that final polish!

Mattilda Bernstein Sycamore was my comrade-in-arms from start to finish. A million panicked phone calls later, girl, it's done! Thank you for everything, up to and including the owl card.

Rebecca Brown, Christine Evans, Kiera Coffee, Michael Cunningham, Fanny Howe, Sikivu Hutchinson, Martin Hyatt, Lisa Jarnot, Kevin Killian, Stacey Levine, Melinda Lopez, Dinaw Mengestu, John McGrath, Eileen Myles, Wendy C. Ortiz, D. Travers Scott, Stephen Soucy, Michelle Tea, Jeremy Tiang, Lidia Yuknavitch: writers/pals/profane illuminators. Thank you.

Montana Ray and CJ Hauser went, seemingly overnight, from being my stellar students to startlingly talented peers. Thanks to both of you, and especially to Montana and Natalie Peart for hosting early iterations of *Bhopal Dance* in their BLT Salon.

Eleanor Bader, Julie Laffin, Sonya Leathers, Carrie Nedrow, Carlos León-Ojeda, Nina Miller, Theresa Senft, and Penelope Treat are just some of the many friends who keep me going and keep me writing. Stephen Trask: a trillion thanks. Most special of special thanks to bestie Frances Sorensen for all the love and cheerleading over all these years!

Thanks to all my wonderful colleagues at Georgetown University, and for the institutional support with which you have provided me. Special thanks to the Georgetown Prison Outreach Project, and I suppose the Arlington County Jail (may it and all prisons evaporate).

It all began on Eastern Island, and ended at Vermont Studio Center. Thank you for these artist residencies that helped me complete this project.

Finks, Feldmans, and Sohns: My extensive extended families all deserve thanks. Your love is my love, just like that '70s song said. And to my grandparents: Adina Lewis, Harold Lewis, Benjamin Fink, Rebecca Fink, zikhronah livrakah.

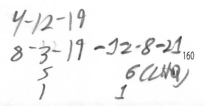